Praise for Louise Doughty

'*The novel's satisfactions lie in the taut prose, the voices of the characters, and the way Doughty uses a tired formula to satirise sentimental notions about country life*'
INDEPENDENT

'*A subversive tale – a wolf in sheep's clothing*'
THE LITERARY REVIEW

'*Clever and diverting*'
TIMES LITERARY SUPPLEMENT

'*Doughty proves she's a confident teller of tales. There are substantial changes of mood and pace, and the novel's humour and ease of digestion belie the affecting sadness and pessimism at it's heart*'
TIME OUT

Honey-Dew

Louise Doughty

Scribner

First published in Great Britain by Touchstone, 1998
This edition published by Scribner, 1999
An imprint of Simon & Schuster Ltd
A Viacom Company

Simon & Schuster
Africa House
64–78 Kingsway
London WC2B 6AH

Simon & Schuster Australia
Sydney

A CIP catalogue record for this book is available from the British Library

ISBN 0-684-82090-0

Printed and bound in Great Britain by
Selwood Printing Ltd., West Sussex

For my parents, Avis and Ken

Author's Note

*T*his novel is set in the county of Rutland, which was England's smallest county until 1974, when it was amalgamated with Leicestershire. After a sustained campaign, it became a county again on April 1st 1997.

Ashpit Spinney and the village of Nether Bowston are both fictional, although other towns, villages and landmarks are real. All shops, restaurants and commercial premises are entirely fictional. The *Rutland Record* is a fictional newspaper, although I have made free use of the generous help given to me by the staff of the two real local papers, the *Rutland Mercury* and *Rutland Times*.

Rutland was remarkably free of serious crime until 1993, when a double murder occurred in one of the villages. Another murder took place in 1996. I would like to stress that the story in this book is in no way based on either of those or on any other real-life cases and any similarities are coincidental.

All characters in this book and the events that happen to them are my own invention – the sole exception is the reference to the strange accidental death of Catherine Noel in 1700, which is a matter of historical record.

Your pipe is drawing sweetly, the sofa cushions are soft underneath you, the fire is well alight, the air is warm and stagnant. In these blissful circumstances, what is it that you want to read about?

Naturally, a murder.

George Orwell
Decline of the English Murder

1

Mankind doesn't need Art, what he needs is stories.

G. K. Chesterton

*I*t was four days before the bodies were discovered, by which time Mr Cowper had begun to mottle. He was lying underneath the kitchen window, where the sunlight caught him every afternoon. Sunlight and corpses do not mix.

Mrs Cowper fared somewhat better, having fallen in the hallway, which was shaded and much cooler.

Springtime came as a surprise. It had been the gloomiest of winters. We had even been denied the consolatory dramas of heavy rain or a snowstorm. Our village can usually look forward to being cut off at least once a year; the roads round here are terrible. Instead, the winter was grey – an endless, anaesthetising grey. For almost all of January and February, the days hardly seemed to break; it was simply that the nights thawed a little during the course of each morning, before hardening again mid-afternoon. I drove down the country lanes to work each morning, radio on, past fields where the soil was sullen. I glanced upwards through the grimy windscreen of my car and thought how heavy the outlook seemed to be, how oppressive the density of the cloud cover.

It was March before a little weak sun bled through, as if the cumuli were a huge swathe of bandaging folded haphazardly across the great wound of the sky.

Warmer weather finally arrived in April, with a suddenness which implied it should be mistrusted. I was worried that we might get a late frost and couldn't decide whether or not to

1

put in some early potatoes – there was nothing in the patch except for a couple of brussel plants which had over-wintered there in ugly splendour. In the end, I decided not to bother. I find it hard to get excited about vegetables.

Instead, while two of my neighbours were swelling, gently, I took advantage of the lighter evenings to enjoy my flowers.

I think back to that time now and wonder what I was doing, what I was trying to grow, as their bodies became less and less human and more and more corpse-like. Logically, I know that death occurs in an instant. One minute you are a subject, the hero or heroine of your own particular story: the next, you are a thing, an object which can be acted upon by anyone who has access to you. You can be lifted, carried, dissected. You can be ignored.

I know it's stupid – call it a guilty conscience, perhaps – but I can't help feeling that while I weeded my borders during the course of that week, the Cowpers were becoming more and more dead, and that if someone had discovered them earlier, they would have been less so. As it was, they were found on the Friday morning because a council workman noticed that they hadn't put their wheely bin out.

We are religious about wheely bins round here. Every Friday, you can see them standing sentinel outside each cottage. People in this village may not speak to their neighbours for years, but we all walk past each other's wheely bins on a weekly basis and are intimate with how worn they are looking, whether any wheels are missing or what might protrude from underneath the lids. Miss Crabbe next door, for instance, fills hers with newspaper.

I fill mine with garden refuse. I was filling it that week, trying to clear the profusion of weeds which was threatening to spoil the previous year's efforts. The narcissi were out already, which was nice. I like them much more than daffodils; their pale faces in the twilight, the scent. I had some tulips as well, apple-dawn red, but my favourites were the wallflowers. They smelt so wonderful after rain – the texture of their petals was of such soft depth. I wonder if I was weeding around my wallflowers as Mr and Mrs Cowper cooled in their cottage that Monday evening.

I wonder if I was considering my arabis, what good ground cover it made, as their bodies stiffened on the Tuesday.

Perhaps on the Wednesday I was regarding the heavy heads of the peonies, as Mr Cowper's flesh discoloured in the sun. I often think that peonies make my garden look as if it belongs to an old person. I am only twenty-seven.

Forget-me-nots sow themselves. I might have thought this as Mrs Cowper's bodily fluids drained to her back – she was found lying on her back – or perhaps I was cutting my rose bushes down and praying that I wasn't going to be plagued with mildew. Mildew of one sort or another is my biggest problem.

What is the worst thing I have ever done? I don't know. To be a murderer, you have to have malicious intent, don't you? I have never done a deliberately malicious thing in my life.

My working week had begun as always, at the Magistrates' Court held each Monday morning at Oakham Castle.

The last time I had been there was for the inaugural meeting of the new Rutland County Council, like a wedding with its pomp and ceremony – the councillors in their finery, accompanying wives in suits and hats, the press and other hoi polloi at the back on wooden benches. Things had quietened down since then, although the green and yellow bunting still trembled in the market square.

That morning, it was business as usual. I was there just before ten. The solicitors were already in place and a small gathering of defendants dotted along the benches. The Great Hall is the only place in the county guaranteed to be cool in the hottest of weather – the stone walls exude a medieval chill.

I was wearing my thin black denim jacket and shivered as I stepped out of the inefficient morning.

I glanced over at the defendants as I passed. There was Tim Gordon, again, up on another charge of driving a motor vehicle without insurance or proper licensing. I went to school with Tim and could still remember him at ten years old, plump and friendly, running around the playground clutching a plastic trumpet. We were quite chummy then. By thirteen, our ways had parted, peeling asunder to encircle opposite ends of the educational spectrum. I was studying for O-levels in six different subjects and CSEs in four. Tim was taking Metalwork and General Science. I would still see him occasionally, lurking at the end of the school drive with a bunch of other no-hopers we called the Drongos. He waved sometimes, but adolescence had intervened and my social standing meant I couldn't possibly return his greeting.

Fifty years ago, Tim might have become a farming hand or a gamekeeper's helper, but there's no work for the men around here these days. As far as I know he's always been unemployed. His dad has a junk yard behind their house in Market Overton. I think he helps out there occasionally. It was his eighth or ninth appearance in court. After each one, he would shuffle over and grin in the way that somebody who has known you since you were five can grin. Then he would ask me not to put his name in the paper, so that his parents wouldn't find out. I always told him I'd have to run it past my editor, but he never made it in. His offences were so commonplace they weren't even any use as fillers. Not even the *Rutland Record* needs lineage that badly.

As I walked past he gave me the grimace, anticipating our familiar exchange, sticking his tongue between his teeth and wobbling a large hand from side to side in a jokey wave.

My boss was there, sat solidly on the press bench with the court list spread out before him. He had already removed his jacket and rolled up his sleeves. His arms were folded across

4

his broad chest and his hands tucked into his armpits. He was leaning back and chatting up Gail, the usher.

Doug looked up as I approached. 'All right, m'duck?' his usual Monday morning greeting.

'All right,' I replied. I mouthed hello to Gail and slid onto the bench next to Doug. 'Anything doing?'

Doug pushed a copy of the list across to me, the papers rasping on the bench's wooden surface. 'Nah, Alison, we'll be out by twelve. A couple of assaults and an affray – that mad lot out at Whissendine. Why they don't just shoot each other and have done with it, I don't know.'

It used to irritate me that Doug sat in on the court sessions, until I realised that he did it for his benefit, not mine. Doug had been editor of the *Record* for eighteen years. He had worked on local newspapers in some capacity or other since he left grammar school. He was not in good health and due to retire soon. In the meantime, he liked to feel that there was a bit of pure news reporter in him still, that there was more to his job than overseeing the advertising and making sure the Village Correspondents filed their copy by Wednesday afternoon. He was aching for something big to happen, just once.

I glanced through the court list. Most of the names were familiar. I flipped open my notepad and arched my back, looking up at the dark wooden beams above me, charred bones against the white plaster ceiling. They always made me think of gibbets. I never reconciled the weight of that twelfth century building with the scrupulousness of its modern usage. The morning's business was a matter of plodding through the list, case by case, with all the usual, reductive formality. Any event, however vital, became procedure. The moment of passion – the drunken decision, the flailing fist – drained of all intensity by detail. Most of the cases would be adjourned. The traffic offences would have fines set. It would be more appropriate to our setting, I sometimes thought, if a sobbing villager was dragged before us in chains and sentenced to be hanged for stealing a rabbit.

The door banged open. I looked up and saw the Thomson family shouldering their way into court; livid-faced Mr Thomson, his nervous, clingy wife and Jeremy, their thick-set son. The Thomsons were in continuous feud with the Smarts, another Whissendine family. I'd never quite worked out the precise nature of their differences except that it all went way back and erupted into affray approximately twice a year. For their court appearances, each man donned an ill-fitting suit and was accompanied by an identical, stringy wife. In the dock, they addressed the leading magistrate as 'sir' or 'ma'am', heads bowed respectfully, trying to outdo each other in their courtesy. They never so much as acknowledged each other. They saved the arguments for their home turf.

'All rise!' called Gail, and there was a shuffling and scraping as we scrambled to our feet for the magistrates, two women and one man, who processed forth from an ante-room behind the bench. They seated themselves in a row beneath the expansive wall covered in huge, decorative horseshoes – the collection is one of the town's chief tourist attractions – and the session began.

The *Rutland Record* claims to be England's oldest newspaper, although I think the name has changed over the centuries. It used to be a broadsheet covering corn prices and the activities of the local highwaymen. It went tabloid in the eighties, like everything else, then duly came close to going out of business. At the last minute, it became the subject of that glorious oxymoron of the business world, a friendly takeover. The Shires Periodical Group already owned half the local newspapers in the region and a stock of trade magazines. We became the smallest, the cutest, item on their books. Nobody expected us to make any money. We had been bought as a sort of mascot, or pet. Actually, we turn in a small profit.

Doug opposed the takeover on principle, but even he was forced to concede that it proved beneficial. Pensions and healthcare packages appeared in the staff contracts. There was a sudden influx of office furniture.

That was all before my time, but when I arrived Doug was still fond of remarking that the wooden chairs they had used before *obliged* you to grow fat, so that whichever desk you sat at, you had your own padding.

Gone are the days of clickety-clack, even in Rutland. Production staff send our camera-ready copy by modem to a printer in Grantham, who has the papers delivered back to Oakham in the small hours of the morning. Cheryl once told me that the day the *Record*'s brand new picture scanner arrived, Doug stood in the subs' room while they unpacked it, and wept.

At the time of the Cowper case, there were two and a half reporting staff, counting Doug. I was Chief Reporter, and Cheryl was part-time everything else; Deputy Editor, legal expert, obituarist and Sports Correspondent. Officially, she worked a half-week, but in practice she was far senior to me. On the rare occasions that Doug took a holiday, Cheryl swept in. She fancied herself as something of a matriarch, always telling me I ought to grow my hair and put on some weight while letting Doug know that he ought to lose some of his and get a decent trim. Rumour had it that she and Doug had once been lovers but I found it hard to believe. They were both in their late fifties. She was married to a man in Stamford who was into racehorses. They had three teenage sons. Doug lived alone, a widower.

Our office was perched on the corner of the market place, a minute's walk from the Castle. The production and advertising staff were on the ground floor. Cheryl and I had a first-floor office and Doug sat in isolationist splendour in an attic office opposite the junk room we call the Library. On market day in summer, it was possible to throw open the sash windows and pick up local gossip and potential stories as they drifted up from the stallholders and customers, floating skywards amongst the hoarse, disinterested cries of 'Peaches ten for a pound' and 'Twenty half o'mush'.

After an hour and a half, I left the court session. The rest of it was going to be a series of non-appearances and adjournments. Doug would stay in case anything unexpected came up – and he was thinking of buying a caravan from Gail's brother and wanted to have a chat with her about it.

There wasn't much for that week's paper. We were all sick of Independence stories and so were the readers. We wanted something fresh to cover but were all too knackered to go out and find it. I needed to get on the phone.

Each Monday, I put a call through to my friend Bill at the fire station and he tells me if anything has happened over the weekend. It was Bill who fed me the bananas, my first story for the *Record*, one small paragraph which is now framed and hanging on my kitchen wall.

> *Missing Bananas*
> *A Belmesthorpe farmer made a surprise discovery on Tuesday morning when he happened upon sixty-three boxes of bananas which had been dumped in one of his fields. An appeal has been made for the owner to come forward. 'We're baffled,' a police spokesperson has admitted.*

When my brother Andrew saw the story he said, 'Oh, for God's sake . . .'

'What's wrong?' I asked.

'The title,' he said. 'It wasn't the *bananas* which were missing, it was the owner. Everybody knew exactly where the bananas were.'

Andrew has always been a pedant.

During the week, all I need to do is keep my ears open. The fire station is a hundred yards down the High Street. I can hear the siren as it starts up. I go to the window and watch to see which way the engine is going, then get on the phone to the Village Correspondents in that direction and get them to look out of their windows too. If I guess right, the engine can be tracked halfway across the county.

As I crossed the Castle grounds I thought that I should ring the Whissendine Correspondent and find out if there were any rumours about the latest fracas between the Thomsons and the Smarts. I wouldn't be able to use any background until after the trial but it would be good to get a few notes done in advance.

The only flurry of excitement in court that morning had been over one of the assault cases, an Oakham man in a suede jacket, up for punching his girlfriend. Just before his case was called, the door opened and a thin young man about my age sidled into the court. Everybody paused as he was approached by Gail. (Sometimes we get tourists coming to have a look around who don't realise that the Castle is closed on Mondays and Gail has to usher them out. We had three Japanese once. It took quite a while to explain.) After a short exchange, Gail gestured the newcomer towards the press bench. He walked swiftly across the court, head down, trying to be as inconspicuous as possible – which made him riveting to watch. He crossed the bench behind us, then slid in next to me. The bench crackled.

Doug is not the sort to waste time on social niceties. He leant forward across me.

'Who are you?' he hissed to the young man.

'David Poe,' he whispered back. 'Press Agency.'

The nationals had descended en masse for Independence, chortling into their notepads and churning out stories that made us sound like characters from an Ealing comedy. The following day, they all disappeared, vultures who had got wind of a fresher carcase.

'What are you doing here?' Doug hissed, ignoring the swift glances from the magistrates' bench. I pressed myself back to facilitate the exchange.

'This Browning,' David Poe replied, indicating the man in suede, who was talking to his solicitor. 'Rumour has it he's a friend of a cousin of Jeremy Beadle. *The Star* are interested.'

Doug let out a short but resonant laugh, his head snapping back and his mouth opening in an exhalation of derision which echoed round the hall. Heads in the courtroom turned. Gail stepped towards us, frowning, and Doug lifted the flat of his hand, nodding an apology.

The friend of the cousin of Jeremy Beadle had finished talking to his brief, a black-suited woman who, while she talked, had been tidying up a scattering of pens and pencils on the table in front of her and pushing them into a plastic pencil case in the shape and design of a packet of Walkers Crisps. She rose to address the Bench, asking for an adjournment for probation reports to be obtained. The adjournment was granted and a date set. Bail remained unconditional.

As Browning turned to leave the court, David Poe eased himself from the bench and sidled out, following.

Doug leant sideways towards me, arms still folded. 'He'll have a fine time if he tries to doorstep that Browning,' he muttered from the side of his mouth. 'He's liable to get a punch up the bracket.'

As I crossed the empty market square half an hour later, I saw David Poe standing in the doorway of the Nearly New shop, looking as though a punch up the bracket might have been exactly what he'd got. He was frowning and muttering and slapping a mobile phone. I stopped and watched him for a moment, unable to resist the temptation to be helpful.

'Excuse me,' I called across the square. He looked up, still frowning. He was sitting next to me a minute ago, I thought. Now he can't even remember who I am, the pillock. His fringe was too long and his hair fell forward over his face, obliging him to make small, sideways tossing motions with his head which added to his air of irritation.

'There's a pay phone right there.' I pointed back towards the butter cross, where the red telephone box stood out like a beacon among the stone buildings. He nodded, still frowning, then broke into an unexpected smile, as if he had just caught sight of himself in my eyes. He lifted the mobile phone in one hand and shrugged. 'Thank you,' he called.

As I opened the door to the office, I wondered whether I should have invited him in to use our phone – but I knew Doug would be back soon, and if David Poe thought Mr Browning was truculent he had yet to witness a full demonstration of Doug's contempt for the national press.

Our biggest fear at the *Record* was that something newsworthy would happen on a Thursday afternoon when the paper was going to press. When a Tornado jet from the RAF base at South Luffenham crashed into Quakers Spinney last autumn, it timed its immolation to coincide with the end of the working day and the last copy of the *Record* rolling off the printer's press in Grantham. Worst-case scenario.

Doug had to make an on-the-spot decision. If we were going to re-write the front page he would have to ring the printer, tell him to pulp every paper and stop his staff going home. All he had was a report of an explosion from the Correspondent in Ayston. Doug was cautious by nature but I think something must have got to him with that one, some tingling in the fingertips perhaps. Cheryl and I were making ready to get our coats on when he appeared in the doorway and announced, 'Something's broke at Ayston. I can smell it.'

He rang the printer from my phone. 'Pulp the lot of them,' he said. 'We'll have the new pages by midnight.'

It paid off. The two-man crew of the Tornado had been killed and a crater twenty foot deep left in the charred forestry. A Ridlington family out on a picnic was missing. It made the *Nine O'Clock News* that night, albeit in the summary.

The family turned up safe and sound the next day but it didn't spoil Doug's professional satisfaction. We had scooped every local paper for miles.

If something big happens on a Friday, there's nothing we can do. By then, the *Record* has been delivered to hundreds of homes across the county and is stacked neatly in every newsagent. We sit glumly at our desks with the weary feeling that the weekend ought to have started. Everybody feels like a day off after press day – but there's next week's paper to fill. We can't afford to leave it all until Monday.

A big story breaking on a Friday is something of a relief. It wakes everybody up for a start, and gives us plenty of time to do the background before we have to go to press.

This story, my story, the murder of the Cowper family, began that Friday.

I was still at home but about to leave for the office. I hate rushing around in the mornings, so I always get up early. I have a bath and play with the water. My Friday morning treat is to do it without the radio on, so I don't have to listen to the news. It is the only concession I make to having put the paper to bed the day before.

My first intimation that something was about to start happening came as I was standing at my kitchen window, finishing my third mug of tea. I often stand there in the mornings, leaning forward against the sink, looking out at the rose bushes in the narrow border between my front aspect and the lane. I like planning things that way. I like planning more roses.

I was clutching my mug in both hands and wondering if I

had cut the bushes back a bit too far. My favourite moment of the gardening year is when the first tiny red shoots appear.

It was then that I heard the vehicle speeding down Brooke Road, some way distant but approaching rapidly. It didn't sound like a car – it was something heavier, the engine shifting gear. I knew immediately that this meant something. Nothing ever speeds through Nether Bowston. It isn't on the way to anywhere.

It was an ambulance, swaying smoothly down the narrow road, with no flashing light or siren. It was followed closely by a police car, also silent. I put down my cup and picked up my bag from the kitchen table. I slammed the front door behind me and was rooting in the bag as I went down the stone path to my gate. The notepad was in my hand as I rounded the corner by Ostlewaite's Barn.

At the end of the road, there was a large detached cottage built of clean red brick. It was one of the few red-brick buildings in the village and always looked very new, perhaps because it was so immaculate. The front lawn was a neat, borderless rectangle, the driveway a short sweep of sandy-coloured shingle. The five-barred gate was creosoted, and, as far as I remember, always closed. I could recall nodding to the middle-aged couple who lived there. They had a daughter, I thought; I wasn't sure. The house was on the edge of the village, the last house on a road that led out to open fields. They were not a family that mixed.

There was no sign of them. The ambulance and police car had parked on the verge. Three other patrol cars were parked in a line further down the road. The ambulance's back doors were open but the paramedics seemed inactive, standing with their arms folded, talking to one of the officers surrounding the cottage.

The front door of the cottage was also open. I could see several bulky, dark figures in the hallway. One of them was bending down.

I was looking at the house as I approached and nearly walked into the line of tape that two officers were stretching across the road, reaching from a sapling on the right-hand side to a fence post on the left. I stopped, momentarily confused that my way should be barred. One of the policemen looked up from affixing his end of the tape. He was a thick-set, middle-aged man with a solid, hard expression. I knew most of the local force but I didn't know him. He gazed at me briefly, then shook his head.

I peered past him to try and see an officer I recognised. Somebody would tell me what was going on.

It was a muggy day, that day. All week, the mornings had been gloomy, the afternoons sunny and the nights dense and close. The pattern had shown no signs of breaking and despite a slight breeze, the clouds seemed bunched up in the birdless sky, as if pressure from elsewhere was squeezing them together. The air felt thick, warm without being comfortable. It was a morning that held no trace of brightness.

An officer emerged from the house and paused on the doorstep, then rested a hand on the door-frame for balance while he lifted a foot and examined the sole of his shoe.

I glanced behind me. Nobody else from the village had come down. I was the first on the scene. I remember thinking, it's not like me to hesitate.

2

The fair breeze blew, the white foam flew,
The furrow followed free;
We were the first that ever burst
Into that sunless sea.

Samuel Taylor Coleridge
The Rime of the Ancient Mariner

*I*t was summer. Gemma was sitting on the low red-brick
wall at the back of her parents' house, perched sideways
with the soles of her bare feet lying flat against the wall's
rough surface. Her head was twisted so that she could look
out over the fields.

The land behind their house was fallow, a lumpy expanse
of ploughed, dark soil in which the occasional pale weed
struggled. She had a vague memory of cows when she had
been small – huge-tongued creatures with wet, yellow-rimmed
eyes that stared back at her without expression. There were
no cows now.

The position she sat in was uncomfortable – there was
nothing to lean against. So after a while she turned her head
away from the fields and rested her chin on her knees. She
examined her toenails.

The previous day, her parents had gone out and left her
alone for over an hour. She had sneaked into her mother's
room and stolen an old red nail varnish from the vanity unit,
then painted her toenails in her bedroom with the door shut.
It was only after they had dried, as she wiggled her feet in
the air, that she thought to return the varnish and look for

remover. There was none. In a panic, she had tried to scrape the varnish off with tissue. It was dry but not hard and came away in smears and lumps. She used one of her own emery boards to slough off the rest but rims of tell-tale red still lingered in the cuticles.

When her parents came home, her father had called up the stairs, 'We're back! What have you been doing?'

'Working on my history project,' she had called down. Then she had shut her bedroom door and changed into trousers and socks.

Now, she examined the toenails up close, the ridged and roughened surfaces, the guilty lividity of the remaining varnish. She picked off a few flakes with her fingernail.

Alongside her right foot, a tiny red ant was making its way across the top of the harsh, hot wall. She watched its progress as it tumbled into the minute black craters which peppered the surface of the brick, flipping itself out of each one without difficulty but still taking several seconds to scurry the length of her foot.

Her long hair felt heavy down her back. She could feel the sun on her head.

She squashed the red ant with one finger.

The History of Murder in England
by Gemma Cowper
Set II – Mr Donaldson
Introduction

Murder is undoubtedly the worst thing you can do to anyone, so it does seem funny that so many people like it so much in that they watch a lot of television programmes and read many books on the subject. A lot of things which are not so bad are taken a great deal more seriously, such as burgling houses and stealing a car and hitting your wife, which everybody agrees are bad things to do. It is only in the case of murder that you get so many films and books.

This is probably for several reasons.
1. Because it is so bad makes it hard to take seriously,
i.e. the very thing that makes it bad also makes people
want to talk about it a lot.
2. People who write books and make television pro-
grammes need to do things that people will want to
watch and for that then things have to happen.
3. Some people do not perhaps realise how awful it is
because the people who it has been done to are never
around to tell their side of the story.

This project will look at some of the worst murders
that have happened in the past in England and ask why
they are often treated so lightly today. A good example
is the Jack the Ripper case. Nobody knows who Jack
the Ripper really was but people are always trying to
work it out whereas very few people are interested in
his unfortunate victims. Also, that is one case where
people make a lot of jokes a lot of the time.

Have people's attitudes changed or has it always been
like this?

What is the current situation?

Will things change in the future?

History and English were her favourite subjects. She was
going to do both at A-level but the third subject was a bit of
a problem. Her father wanted her to do a science because he
said that it was important she should do something he could
really help her with. He was keen to help. He had already put
together a revision programme for her GCSEs. It was pinned
to the kitchen wall, with each weekday evening marked out
as a colour block; red for History, blue for English, green
for Geography and so on (the colour codes were drawn in
at the bottom). She was doing ten subjects, so if she revised
for one each evening, Monday to Friday, it would take two
weeks to get through them all before the rota came round

again. Saturdays were for gaining what her father called 'a general overview'. Sundays were a day of rest and clarinet practice.

She couldn't wait for A-levels. She couldn't wait to not have to think about photosynthesis or coastal shelving. She knew that when the details of the ordinary world had been left behind, she could be as brilliant as she deserved to be. Nobody had fully realised her potential as yet – not even her father.

English Language and Literature were well in hand already so she was permitting herself to read ahead. She had consulted Mrs Macpherson on what would be on the A-level syllabus next year and Mrs Macpherson had said, 'The Romantic poets, Gemma. But I wouldn't bother yourself with those right now. You've got quite enough on your plate.' Gemma had nodded, glowing with the knowledge that she was going to do something above and beyond what she was supposed to do. By the time it came to Next Year, she would be way ahead.

Friday, 17th May 1996
Today was even hotter than it has been up till now and by lunch time I thought, God, I will never complain about being cold again. The only cool place on the whole planet was English because that block was built centuries ago and the stone walls are so thick that nothing can get through. I find it very boring that we are still stuck on Ted Hughes. Everybody else seems really into dead dogs in ditches and I just think, been there, done that, got the t-shirt. Jane and Biz are very fond of calling me Gemma Cowpat right now which they seem to think is hilarious, as if we didn't go through that one in the first year. I am a little clod surrounded by pebbles. They are all just completely stupid. I think I should tell them that my name is Klopstock and I will

18

*one day defy the whole of England. Not that it would
mean anything to them.*

*Dad had another one of his talks with me today.
He explained why it is best for me to bring my essays
downstairs and do them at the dining table where he
can keep an eye on me. I reminded him that the reason
I am allowed to work in my room is because of Mum
watching the television and he said that was why he
had told her she couldn't any more and if she wanted
something to do she could help us. I can't imagine why
he thinks Mum is going to be any help. It was on the
tip of my tongue to remind him about the talk we had
the other weekend when he explained how Mum isn't
our intellectual equal and we mustn't expect too much
of her but he wasn't in the mood to be reminded of
something he had said before.*

Gemma closed her notebook. She was in her bedroom,
recovering.

She had been sitting on the wall picking at her toenails
when her father had come out and called to her. She had
turned but the sun was in her eyes and all she could see
was a blur of white which hurt the inside of her head. Her
father's voice came from the blur. 'Gemma. Come inside.
Come inside now.'

She swung her legs down to the ground and stood, unsteadily.
As she walked down the garden, towards the blur, pale
colours grew, like in a developing photograph. Her father
was standing with his hands on his hips and the stance
separated the two sides of his blue shirt, revealing a flat,
pale stomach. He was wearing his trousers and slippers, but
no socks.

When she reached the patio, he stepped forward to meet
her. She stopped. He placed his hands on her shoulders.

'Look at me,' he said.

She looked at him.

'Look me in the face.'

She looked, and felt the same dull hurt inside her head that she had felt when she looked at the sun. The cool shade of the patio was making her skin prickle and she had pins and needles in her left foot.

He shook his head slowly. 'Gemma, Gemma, Gemma . . . you are such a dreamy thing.' His voice had taken on the soft quality that she hated so much. She did not know why she hated it. When he used it, she wanted to look at the ground. She wanted a gaping hole to appear in the patio, one large enough for her to fall down, like Alice in Wonderland.

'I've *told* you . . .' the soft voice insisted. 'I've told you that if you sit in the sun like that you will get a headache. Haven't I told you?'

She nodded.

He sighed, an ineffably sad sigh, as if she could never begin to understand the breadth of his love for her, a love so wide that it encompassed even the distant blazing sun. 'Go inside to recover, like a good girl.' He chuckled indulgently. 'And next time remember.'

She made a minute motion with her shoulders to indicate that she was turning to go, but he did not remove his hands. There was a pause. She did not like to examine his face in detail; the slight fair stubble, the porous nose; so she concentrated on his large, liquid grey eyes. If you looked at somebody's eyes for long enough, you could forget that you were looking at a person.

'What would you do if I weren't here to look after you?' he said. 'What would happen to you? I can't begin to imagine.'

Up in her bedroom, she opened her diary and read the last entry, then she closed the notebook and put it down. She went to the window.

Her bedroom looked out over the road. They were the last house in the village, so nobody ever came down the road. She didn't like watching it, because nobody ever came down it.

There was only the spotless driveway and an unchanging row of trees.

This side of the house was sunlit, bleached. The shadow of their front gate was a black parallelogram against the pale gravel.

Chapter 3

Now that we have considered some historical examples, it is perhaps worth considering cases where the facts are less certain. It is a matter of record that Earl Ferrers killed his servant because he was a peer of the realm and it was enormously important a peer being hung like that. Some historians have suggested that it even prevented a revolution in England similar to those that had occurred in Europe. Had Earl Ferrers been as ordinary as his victim, however, then we might never know about it today. It is always worth bearing in mind that there must be thousands of murders that have never come to light.

Even among the aristocracy, strange things have happened which cannot always be explained. Take the case of teenager Catherine Noel, although she would not have been called a teenager in those days.

On Boxing Day in 1700, the Noel family of Exton Hall, who still exist today, held a grand ball. Catherine Noel, daughter of the family, played Juliet in a production of Romeo and Juliet *which was made up for the entertainment of those attending the ball. In the scene where Juliet takes the poison, Catherine mimed taking it then swooned, and the musicians at the ball played a lament as she was lowered into a family chest and the lid put on. When the play was over, everybody*

21

applauded and waited for Catherine to get up out
of the chest. When she didn't, they applauded again.
Eventually, somebody went to lift the lid and found
that it was jammed shut. By the time they got the lid
off, Catherine had suffocated.

Nobody can be exactly sure what happened in this
case and everyone who has written about it has said
that it was just a tragic accident and that her parents
were terribly upset, not to mention all the other guests
at the ball.

However, can we be really sure of what happened
here?

It was during exams that her father instigated the 'early-to-bed' programme. It was essential, he said, that she got a good night's sleep, otherwise she would not be able to perform.

She found it difficult going to bed early in the summer. Her curtains were made of fine cotton in a pale blue and white stripe. They haemorrhaged daylight. She would lie wide awake on her narrow bed watching the curtains, motionless but furiously restless, waiting for the light to fade.

Tuesday, 7th July 1996
It's been weird since exams finished. The mornings are
really weird. I wake up expecting to feel great but I
don't. I deliberately don't set my alarm just to see what
happens but I wake up at the usual time and am always
wide awake immediately, planning all the things that I
think I have to do. When I realise I don't have to do
them any more, I feel quite upset. I make myself feel
better by thinking about Coleridge and how sad he was.
You would think that having mastery of the pneumonic
would make somebody happy. Most people, after all,
don't even know what a pneumonic is, let alone have
mastery of it. (Most people probably think it is a bad

cold!) Yet he was a really unhappy person. It made me wonder whether even when my results come through, it won't be enough for me. Sometimes I think it would be quite nice just to be ordinary. Last Saturday, I went with Dad to the Co-op and as we drove through Oakham I saw Clare walking past the library wearing a top that was too skinny for her, with a big flappy collar and the arms really tight. It was black, and the collar had a green stripe. Even though it was a really stupid top, she looked really good and cool because of the way she was walking and holding her head and because of who she is, I suppose. I know for certain that I could wear exactly the same top and just look stupid. Although I bet she doesn't know what a pneumonic is!

Weirdly, though, she also writes poetry. We got talking in the library during revision and she showed me something she had written. It was pretty stupid, all about flowers and leaves, and I think she thought it was a sonnet when it wasn't. At the bottom, she had written copyright, and signed it and she said I should do the same with all mine in case somebody stole them.

The morning that her results were due, she woke early. She sat on the end of her bed, from where she could open her curtains a crack, and watched the stillness of their front garden, the quietness of the road. She waited for the postman to come down the road.

When he did, she ran downstairs, picked up the buff-coloured envelope and took it to where her father sat at the dining table. The breakfast things had been laid out; the oval place-mats, the jug of milk, the patterned cereal bowls – but nobody had eaten anything. Her father was sitting at his place, not speaking. Her mother was in the kitchen.

Gemma stood shyly in front of her father. It was always the way – school reports, anything. She had never been allowed to open the envelopes herself. She had to stand in front of her father while he did, waiting, watching his face for an interpretation of what he was reading.

For some time, her father's face did not change. He laid the papers from the examination boards out on the table, where they rocked slightly. He looked from one to the other.

Gemma's arms were by her sides. She could feel her fingers trembling. She waited for his face to crack, or flicker – anything that would give some indication.

Eventually, he rose from his seat.

He would not look at her. He half turned towards the door, then said, softly, 'I have never been more ashamed in my life.' He left the room.

Gemma felt flushed with heat. She went and stood behind her father's empty chair, gripping it. She read the results.

She had fail grades in every subject except Geography, for which she had received a C.

Her father only referred to her results once after that, about three days later. He had still not spoken to her. She had spent most of her time in her room, only emerging when her mother called her down for meals.

She was leaving the kitchen, carrying a glass of milk. Her father was in the hall.

She stopped. It might be possible to ease past him without him noticing – he had his back to her, fastening his coat – but if he turned she would be trapped against the wall. She hesitated. Perhaps she should go back into the kitchen or through to the dining room until he had gone – but then, if he was aware of her presence, that would seem a bit peculiar.

Suddenly, without turning round, he spoke. 'I am going to visit your headmaster,' he said evenly, 'to demand an explanation.'

The full humiliation of her failure washed over her. Her

father was actually going to demand that the school explain why she had done so badly. He was going to have her inadequacy spelt out for him, word by word. She had to say something, to stop him.

'Is that . . . They probably don't know . . .' she faltered.

He turned to face her. Underneath his coat, he was wearing a jacket and tie, smartly layered despite the summer heat outside. He looked at her. 'You don't imagine that I am going to let this pass?' he said calmly.

She glanced down at the carpet, then back up at him. His face was kindly and resolute, and she saw with a wash of horror that he did not actually believe her examination results. He thought there had been some mistake. He thought that he could sort things out.

She was agonised for him. She opened her mouth, but he raised a hand to stop her. 'My dear,' he said, 'you must trust me.' He left.

She went back into the kitchen, still clutching her milk, and watched him as he strode confidently down the gravel drive and opened the gate. He got into the car, closing the door behind him with an efficient *thunk*. He fastened his seatbelt before he started the engine, as he always did, and backed out of the drive slowly and with great care. She noticed that he did not lower the car window despite the heat. She thought, he is like a spaceman or an alien, going off in his sealed craft, off into a world which he doesn't understand. She realised that she knew more about that world than her father. At least she went to school each day, during term time. Her father had not worked since taking early retirement two years ago. (Her mother had explained that his employers did not understand how stressful his position was – he had been a manager for an oil company in Leicester).

Gemma realised that it was now her job to protect her father, and her mother. She would have to look after them both.

Her father did not return for some hours, and when he did, he went straight up to the bedroom and did not emerge for two days. Her mother said to her, over breakfast on the second morning, 'Your father's poorly.'

It was her mother who told her that she would not be returning to school when the new term began. Her father had decided it was a waste of money.

'But what about my A-levels?' Gemma said. Her voice sounded squeaky in her own ears, disbelieving.

'Your father says you can study for them at home if you want. He can help you. You can send away for study packages. He read an article about it in the paper.'

20th November 1996
Sometimes I can't believe it's November already. The weather is horrible and it will be Christmas before we know it. Mum let me go to the shop for two pints of milk this morning, while Dad was out. She said it was time I got some fresh air. There is a new man in the shop now. I don't know what has happened to the old one. I don't even know when he got replaced. The new man said hello in a friendly sort of way but he probably didn't know I live round here. As I was leaving, I saw the Christmas cards on the shelf and I could hardly believe it. At school, everybody will be writing out cards. I used to think it was really stupid the way we all sent cards to each other when we could just say Happy Christmas but I suppose we had all got into the habit. You could always tell who was most insecure because they gave their cards out really early so that you had plenty of time to buy them one. Heather with the lisp would give hers out the first week back after half term.

I don't expect I will get many this year. I rang a couple of people last week, even though Dad doesn't like me using the phone because of the bill and comes and puts the egg timer next to me on the stairs. I didn't have much to say to them anyway. Jane told me a few things about school but I didn't really have anything to say back.

Dad is getting more and more perculiar. He sits in the chair all morning and reads the paper. Sometimes, he gets really excited. He will jump up and wave the paper around and talk about taking action. Sometimes he will write a letter or get on the phone or go out. Sometimes he is like this all afternoon. Then, in the evenings, he is very quiet. He is often quiet for a couple of days. He has rung the electrical shop and told them to come and take the telly back because he says it is corrupt and we've got to economise.

I asked him once about the idea about me doing A-levels at home and he said he was seeing to it, but then nothing ever happened. I thought maybe he would think I should do some re-takes or something at the sixth form college, but we never got around to talking about that either. I am still reading my Coleridge and have discovered a poet called John Clare who is, if anything, even better. Both of them are much better than Wordsworth who just drones on and on for pages and I can't believe that everyone thinks he is the great poet. Apparently, Coleridge thought so too which is why he was depressed a lot of the time. I find it reassuring that even Coleridge thought he was no good sometimes!

John Clare is in one of the anthologies that I took out from the school library. I'm surprised they haven't written wanting their books back as I've got loads of them, but I'm very glad as I'm not sure how I would get hold of any more. I asked Dad to give me a lift into Oakham last week so I could go to the town library

*but all he would say is that he would some time soon.
It's ages since we've been to town. I wonder if they
will be putting Christmas decorations up yet. Last year
the old-fashioned coloured bulbs across the High Street
looked great but the big plastic Father Christmas's on
the lampposts looked stupid.*

Her mother's birthday was in January. Gemma bought her
a card from the village shop, a large one wrapped in loose
cellophane that crinkled when the man in the shop slipped it
inside the brown paper bag. There was nothing suitable for a
present, so Gemma asked her father for a lift into Oakham on
the Saturday before, so that she could go and buy something.
Her father said, not to worry, he would get something for
her, and came back with a china box with four large holes
in the gilt-edged lid. Inside was pot-pourri.

Her father seemed in a good mood. As he handed Gemma
the box he said, 'Do you know what I nearly got your
mother?' He paused, as if there was a possibility that Gemma
might guess. Then he said, 'A budgerigar. I nearly bought
your mother a budgie.' Then he laughed out loud.

Her mother's birthday fell on a Wednesday. In the morning,
Gemma went down early and laid out the breakfast things,
adding her gift, which she had wrapped in the paper her father
had bought – paper so wafery thin it was almost translucent.
She had had to wrap the present twice.

Her father came down and went past her into the kitchen,
humming. He emerged a few minutes later with a tray on
which there were three of their best crystal glasses and a
carton of pink grapefruit juice. 'I don't think your mother's
ever had this,' he said proudly. 'It's like ordinary grapefruit
juice but sweeter.'

They sat waiting for some time. Her father became a little
impatient, whistling and muttering under his breath. 'Where's
she got to . . . ?' His own present to her sat on the other side

of her place-mat. From its shape and bulk Gemma guessed, correctly, that it was a cardigan.

When her mother eventually appeared in the doorway, wearing a grey woollen dress, her father stood up and opened his arms wide and said, 'Ta-da!'

The pink grapefruit juice was a great success. After tasting it, her mother giggled, as if it had made her tipsy.

It was after breakfast that her father made his announcement. He had a surprise. As a special treat, that night, they were going to go out to dinner.

Gemma only had one skirt, a summer one which she had bought from Oakham market the previous year, for £5.99. She could remember fingering the filmy patterned cotton, lilac and orange. The adjacent store sold country & western CDs and was playing 'I'm on a Honky-Tonk Merry-Go-Round'. Gemma mentally counted through the money in her purse, saved from the days when her father gave her pocket money. She could just about do it.

Amazingly, later that afternoon, she saw someone else from school wearing one of the very same skirts, one of the cool sixth-formers called Judy. She had cut a slit up one side and was wearing it with black wool tights and Doc Martens. Gemma felt proud of herself. Maybe she was not quite so useless at clothes after all.

In her bedroom at home, the skirt did not look so cool. Perhaps it was her tan tights and brown loafers.

In the car driving to Oakham, her mother kept saying, 'Well, this is a surprise all right. It certainly is a surprise.'

It was a freezing night and Oakham was deserted. The only person Gemma saw as they drove down the High Street was a man in the telephone box outside the bank. His dog was waiting for him outside, a West Highland terrier wearing a tartan coat, snuffling around with its lead trailing across the pavement.

Round the corner from the market place there was a new Italian restaurant called Mama Mia. It was the first Italian restaurant in town, as far as Gemma knew. It had green paintwork and a wrought-iron lamp hanging above the doorway. In the window, there was a framed menu. They stopped to look.

'I didn't book,' her father muttered anxiously.

Gemma peered through the window. Only two of the tables were occupied, both by couples. The interior of the restaurant was lit by an orange glow so soft and textured that it almost felt warm through the glass. A young man wearing a white apron was standing on the bar and changing the bulb in the light that hung above it. He was talking over his shoulder to someone Gemma couldn't see.

Her parents were silent, examining the menu. She waited beside them, feeling the hardness and coldness of the pavement through the thin soles of her shoes. She had forgotten her gloves and her hands were jammed into the pockets of her duffle jacket. When she exhaled, her breath condensed against the restaurant's window.

Her father shook his head. 'We can't afford this . . .' he murmured. 'Look at this. This is a real rip-off.'

Gemma felt herself freeze over.

Her mother was quiet for a long time. Then she said, 'It is rather pricey . . .'

Gemma turned away and bit the inside of her lip. She was so cold she had to bite hard in order to feel anything. She closed her eyes and clenched her teeth, willing herself to draw blood.

'I tell you what,' her father said eventually. 'It's your birthday, Mum. I tell you what, you and Gemma go in and have something. I'll give you the money. I can get some fish and chips and wait in the car.'

Gemma tightened her fists inside her jacket and thought,

please, Mum, *please*, but even as she thought it, knew what her mother's response would be.

'Oh no, dear, we couldn't possibly do that. No . . .' She tailed off, then suddenly brightened. 'I know, let's all get fish and chips and take them home.'

In the car going home, her mother said, twice, 'We don't often have fish and chips, do we?'

Her father had turned the heating off before they left. He put it on again as soon as they got in but it took a while for the house to warm up. Gemma kept her duffle jacket on while they ate the fish and chips at the dining table, putting the newspaper on the same oval place-mats they used for breakfast.

Ode to Kubla Khan

Oh Kubla Khan! How can you know what
It is like to be a girl trapped as I am
Buried above ground.

Vengeance will be mine!
Who will afford me a shelter when I have broken
free
From the manacles forged by my youthfulness
I am encompassed round by many things but mostly
Mine own inability.

I am fill'd with sorrow
And the sadly followed furrow
Breaths not upon tomorrow
All I can do is burrow –

And I have been buried enough!
                    copyright Gemma Cowper
                    3rd February 1997

23rd March 1997
*Today, I had to think quite hard to work out what day it
was. There doesn't seem much difference between the days
and the weekends now. I was surprised however when I
looked at the date and saw how long it was since I last
wrote in my diary. It seems perculiar that the months are
going by so quickly when the days are so slow.*

*We don't do anything much now and I find it quite
hard to stay interested in my poetry even though I know
I am writing what is some of my best stuff these days.
Coleridge wrote his best stuff when he was depressed as
well, I'm sure. I think it's important that I keep writing
all my thoughts down because you never know when
one might become a poem but it is difficult because
often I just can't remember what I have thought.*

*For he on mildew hath fed
And drunk the scum of paradise.
A thousand thousand slimy things live on, and so do
I.
I am a girl who has penance done and penance more
will do.*

In my opinion, The Ancient Mariner *goes off a bit
when you get to the hermit.*

Suddenly, the weather became hotter. It had been grey for so
long that when the sun broke through, Gemma felt as strange
and as dislocated as if they had moved house. The sun showed
how dusty her bedroom was, bleaching the colour out of her
blue duvet. She felt, all at once, that changes were coming.
One day, she noticed that the huge elder tree in the lane had
broken into eternal green, and she smiled to realise that there
had been a tree in that spot at all. It seemed as surprising as
if she had opened her curtains one morning and found that
somebody had thrown up a block of flats overnight.

The day was punctuated by meals. These were her only points of reference. They still had dinner early, going to bed at the same time her father had arranged when they had all been revising for her GCSEs. During the winter, this had seemed like a good idea – the nights were so dark and miserable and the house was always so cold. But now that spring had arrived, she realised that, again, they would be going to bed when it was still light.

One afternoon, she said to her father, lightly, 'I think I might go for a walk after dinner. Mum said we needed some bread for tomorrow.'

Her father stopped and put down his book. He had taken to reading about the Suez crisis. He had told Gemma that it was important for men like him to understand where everything had gone wrong.

He looked at her, then he sighed. 'Gemma, do you really have no imagination?'

As usual, he paused for some time, as if this was a question she might want to answer.

Eventually, he closed his book and sat up in his chair. 'Gemma, I realise that in some ways I have failed you as a father. I have not been strict enough. I have allowed you to go your own dreamy way about the house, as you do every day, as if it doesn't matter what you do. I, however, do have some imagination. I read the papers every day. If you read the papers every day, you would realise that it is out of the question you going off wandering around the countryside whenever you feel like it.'

He returned to his book.

After the meal, Gemma rose from the table. She rose slowly. She had been doing everything carefully, that afternoon. The windows were all closed and locked now. The windows would always be closed.

As she rose, she had the feeling that her life had gone into slow motion. Her body seemed to straighten in one fluid movement. Her mother was reaching out a creaking hand for the glass of water that sat in front of her. Her father was leaning back in his seat, tipping slowly, easing himself.

As she moved away from the table, she realised that she had become deaf. Perhaps it was because she was moving so slowly. There was no sound from her bare feet on the carpet. The dishes that she held piled in her hands were solid as rock. The kitchen swung towards her as she left the dining room, the jangly whiteness of it widening her eyes.

At this rate, she thought, my life is going to take for ever.

Then, suddenly, there was a rush of noise in her ears, a multiple pile-up of sound. She was standing at the kitchen sink and her hands were immersed in hot, sudded water. The water hurt. Lying beside the sink were her mother's pink, flaccid gloves, and she knew without remembering that she was doing the washing-up with bare hands because the gloves were damp inside. They had been clammy.

The sink was too full. The dishes clattered and tinkled; plates, glasses and cutlery all in together. Soapsuds were clambering up the stainless steel in a last-ditch attempt to escape. The water foamed and fell as she scrabbled in it. When she lifted a plate, she saw that her hands were red and swollen. Water splattered the front of her t-shirt and she felt the warmth of it, then instantly the cold.

Her father was standing beside her, very near, his mouth close to her ear. He was saying something, something about rinsing the plate, but the words were huge and distorted, like a badly tuned radio. He was wearing a short-sleeved shirt, and in the corner of her vision she could see the empty flesh of his upper arms. It was marbled, with a scattering of sparse pale hairs.

Her fingers closed round the next item in the sink. The handle was smooth and weighty. She lifted it.

Her mother had gone into the village to catch the shop before it closed at six o'clock. It was five to six. It was going to be another early night.

Her father's arm grazed against hers. She lifted the knife in her hand.

Even though he wasn't leaning against her, she felt the weight of him, the purity of his love for her, the density of it – and she knew that to be loved that much was no longer bearable. She turned.

3

In 1995, 61% of homicide victims were acquainted with their killer or killers.

Homicide Index
Home Office Research Statistics Directorate

D ID THEY KNOW THEIR KILLER? was one choice, which had pleasingly scary undertones. In a rural area like ours it seemed to imply *you might be next.* HUNT FOR MURDER ORPHAN was another, which I thought had too much pathos. In the end we settled for WHERE IS GEMMA?. The use of the first name would appeal to our readers' familiarity with Nether Bowston and the Cowper family, despite the fact that most people in Rutland had probably never been there or met them. The Cowpers had only lived in the county for twelve years, I discovered, so they were outsiders, but their murder was the first to occur in Rutland this century, which made them very local indeed.

Suddenly, everybody remembered an association with the family. Jennifer in reception? Her mother had been to Keep Fit with Mrs Cowper, years ago. Ken, the man who delivered our stationery supplies from a wholesaler on Ashwell Road? He had been behind the counter once when Mr Cowper came in to get some 100gsm bond and three rolls of fax paper. He knew exactly what it was because Mr Cowper had telephoned in advance to check that they sold goods to the general public and had been very specific about what weight of paper he wanted.

Doug had been for his usual weekend drink in the Westgate

Tavern and got talking to a schoolteacher at the posh school
the daughter went to until last year. The teacher had had some
sort of run-in with Cowper who, he said, was *a right rum sod*.
'I don't think I'd ever met him myself,' Doug ruminated as
he told us this, 'although he might have been that git who
turned up at the council meeting a couple of years ago and
said had we all thought clearly about what independence
would mean for the rates and the educational system was
bad enough round here as it was. I remember him because
they had to throw him out. You were on holiday, Alison.
But he came from Nether Bagwash, this bloke.'

We all wanted to be a part of it. It was our murder.

As it had happened practically on my doorstep, I now had
a certain *cachet*. A special degree of sympathy was extended
towards me, as if the physical closeness of my home to theirs
made me a near-victim. People said things like, 'You must be
terrified'. As they said it, there was envy in their eyes.

Doug urged me to make the most of what he called 'the
personal angle'. He was writing the front page story, but I was
to write a side column entitled THEY LIVED NEXT DOOR.

It was generally agreed that we should have an embargo
on the phrase 'house of horror'. So we ran a picture caption
underneath a large photograph of the Cowpers' place which
said *Shock in* Rutland Record *offices was intensified this
week at the realisation that the tragic murder house was
only minutes' walk away from the home of Chief Reporter
Alison Akenside.* I tried to think of a way of beginning the
report which did not say, *I was first on the scene last Friday*
but realised I was fighting a losing battle. *I was first on the
scene last Friday when police officers made the gruesome
discovery* . . .

There are some occasions when only certain words will do,
when people need the comfort of the inevitable. I could have
written, *I was annoyed when they wouldn't let me through
the police barriers to have a proper nose around* or *What*

struck me most was the officer wiping something off his shoe; but at a time like that, you can't rub people's noses in too much reality. The event was public property, and that demanded that we wrote a collective response. People would turn to us for information phrased in a way that sounded like a common voice, the language of the market place just outside our office door – the same market where you could buy coloured cotton reels and pet food and cheap wooden photo frames complete with picture of blond, smiling cherub (useful if your own kid is plug-ugly).

I had no reason to question what I wrote.

Miss Crabbe, my neighbour, had no such scruples. She caught me at my front gate as I was leaving for a press conference at the local police station on the Tuesday morning.

Nether Bowston had had the busiest three days in its history. Convoys of vehicles had been to-ing and fro-ing down Brooke Road all weekend. I cancelled my Friday night game of badminton with my friend Lizzie and my Saturday hair appointment in Leicester. I spent most of that weekend at one or other of my windows.

The nationals were on the scene by the end of the day. The police had drafted in a super I didn't know – a fat geezer with shiny buttons who combed his hair before he spoke to reporters. He held an impromptu conference in front of the house that evening so he wouldn't have the tabloid snappers crawling round the fields at the back and leaping over garden walls. Further details would be given at the regular Tuesday press conference at Oakham police station but the dailies got enough to run the story. Mr Thomas Cowper (52) and Mrs Edith Cowper (53) had died from multiple stab wounds. The murder weapon had not yet been found. Time of death was not yet established but it had probably happened at the beginning of the week. Police were extremely concerned for the safety of their daughter,

Gemma (17), who was missing. There was no sign of any forced entry.

There are no upstairs windows at the front of my cottage. It is one of the model cottages built by a local benefactor at the turn of the last century. He wanted his tithe workers to have decent housing, but it was considered unseemly that they should be able to look down on any aristocrats who might pass through the village. There is a small upstairs window in the back bedroom. I discovered that if I leant out of it with a pair of binoculars I could just make out the moving shapes of the officers drafted in to search the field behind the Cowpers' house. They were wearing t-shirts and trousers, some had caps and gloves, and they were raking their way slowly across the whole field. I wondered if they got bored after a couple of hours – or was a murder case still so unusual that they stayed alert and keen, eager to be the one to discover a vital clue? Occasionally they would stop and chat to each other. I envied them. I thought it was probably fun.

Onlookers turned up, of course; local people who just happened to be passing through. There was even a couple who had come all the way from Corby. They stopped me as I was walking down the lane on the Sunday morning. Was there a pub nearby where they could get lunch? I told them the only pub in Nether Bowston closed twenty years ago. That out of the way, they wanted to know if I knew where the murder had taken place. I pretended ignorance and walked away, shaking my head at the scope and unsubtlety of human curiosity. What shall we do this morning darling? Oh, I know, let's go and have a look round that village where two people have been viciously slaughtered in their own home.

Miss Crabbe waylaid me as I was unlocking my car on Tuesday morning. I was not in the mood for a gossip. I wanted to write up some notes at the office before I went to the press conference.

'Alison,' she called out to me, raising a white, long-fingered hand and wagging it in my direction. 'Alison, I'm so glad I caught you. I tapped at your door last night but you must have been out.' We both knew I hadn't been out. I had been in the bath. My bathroom is on the ground floor and I have my baths so hot that steam billows out of the window. It almost envelops both our gardens.

I had successfully dodged Miss C all weekend but now my time was up.

'I thought I ought to have a quick word, in the light of recent events,' she continued. 'I suppose we will be covering this one together.'

Miss Crabbe is a flat-chested seventy-something who has lived in the village for ever. I recruited her as Nether Bowston's Correspondent not long after I moved in. (The old one had just died of pneumonia and I was damned if I was going to do it.) Her usual remit included meetings of the women's section of the Royal British Legion, car boot sales and the local annual pancake tossing competition. This year, a Mrs Edward Wright won the Mrs John Burnish Memorial Prize after tossing eight pancakes in one minute. Mrs John Burnish was an unfortunate casualty of the contest five years ago. After a valiant six pancakes, she collapsed and died.

I knew that Miss Crabbe would expect to be included in the coverage of the Cowper case and I had bad news for her. Doug had told me on Friday that he wanted to cover it himself, which meant I was effectively demoted to Village Correspondent, and Miss Crabbe was demoted to your average local busybody.

'I'm afraid not,' I replied, opening my car door and tossing my bag onto the passenger seat. I straightened. She folded her arms and raised both eyebrows. 'Doug is covering it,' I said. 'I'm quite annoyed about it, actually, but you know how he is.' This was true. I was annoyed that I was no longer Chief Reporter the minute anything of interest occurred. It didn't happen often but when it did I couldn't help wondering whether I should defect to the *Leicester Mercury*.

'But won't he want the Village Correspondent's angle . . . ?' Miss Crabbe trailed off, crestfallen.

I got into the car – rude of me while she was still talking, but I was in a hurry. I wound down the window before I slammed the door. 'I'm sort of more or less doing that,' I said out of the window. I started the engine. Then I added, 'Isn't it awful?'

'Oh, *yes*,' she agreed vehemently. 'Terrible. Absolutely awful. In their own home. I do hope they catch him. That poor girl.'

Oakham Police Station was once a pre-fabricated hut with a felt roof and a small car park behind it. Crime has never been big round here. Plastic letters above the doorway used to read PUBLIC ENTRANCE, although for several years the sign was intermittently incomplete. Local lads were in the habit of climbing up under the cover of darkness and removing the L.

Later, we got a proper red-brick police station, just like a grown-up town.

The car park was full and cars were lining both sides of Station Road. Doug and I had walked round from the office. As he lumbered his way past two journalists talking to each other on the steps, one of them murmured to the other, 'Douglas Hartley, edits the local comic.' I wondered what that made me, trotting in his wake; his glamorous sidekick, perhaps.

Inside, the small lobby was full of waiting journalists. The two closest to the door were giggling to each other. 'Plastic ferns,' one was saying, gesturing towards the fake foliage in the red-brick border that rings the lobby. 'Plastic ivy, plastic *yucca*, for God's sake.'

WPC Alexander was standing behind the wooden reception counter.

Doug went up to the counter and leant his elbows on it. 'I'll 'ave half a cider, Carol,' he said to the WPC.

'So will I an' all,' she muttered.

Inspector John Collins arrived. 'Ladies and gentlemen, would you like to come up?'

John normally held his Tuesday morning press call in his office, as his audience usually consisted of Doug, me, three black coffees and a packet of chocolate digestives. With over thirty journalists to accommodate, we were now moved to the officers' recreation room, where rows of chairs had been set out and the pool table pushed up against the wall. When we were all seated, John introduced the fat super in charge of the investigation.

Sixty police officers had been drafted into the county to assist in the search for Gemma Cowper. (The fat super referred to her throughout as 'young Gemma'.) East Midlands Water had donated sonar equipment to help search local beauty spot Rutland Water. RAF divers were expected to join in. Special caterers would be hired to feed the various personnel involved. Many local people had volunteered their help. The response from the public had been overwhelming.

At this, one of the nationals called out, 'What makes you think she's still in the area?' and another replied, 'Shut up 'til he's finished.'

The search would of course be extended nationwide. The longer it went on, the more concerned they were becoming for young Gemma's safety.

Most of us had our heads down while we were making notes. We raised them to look at him when he got to the interesting bit.

There had been a sighting in the area of a young man acting suspiciously the day before the murders were presumed to have taken place. He was described as white, early to mid thirties, with black curly hair, scruffily dressed but with red baggy trousers made of a loose fabric. A photofit would be

43

available later in the day. They were most anxious to trace him in order to eliminate him from their inquiries.

There was also another as yet unconfirmed sighting of someone who might or might not be the same man driving an extremely dilapidated car, make unknown, with a girl answering Gemma's description in the passenger seat.

A thicket of arms was raised at the question and answer session but the response to all queries was more or less the same. It was too early to speculate. Wrapping up, the fat super informed us that he would now hand us over to Inspector John Collins to continue with other local crime. There was a rising hubbub as everyone except Doug and me scrambled to their feet. Those who had seated themselves at the back rushed melodramatically for the door.

'Do you want me to get this?' I asked Doug.

'No,' he said, 'you get back. I want to try and get John on his own, see if I can get anything.'

I was standing on the kerb of Station Road, waiting for cars to pass before I could cross.

'Alison! *Hi!*' From the tone of voice, you might have thought I was being greeted by an old boyfriend from years back, one who had never quite got over me. I turned.

David Poe was standing at the top of the police station steps and waving down at me. He gambolled towards me with that loose-legged, casual motion that very confident people use when going down steps – all four limbs swinging. It always makes me hope they will trip and fall flat on their faces. Other journos glanced at him, then at me. I wondered how he knew my name.

'Hi!' he repeated, with boundless enthusiasm. I pretended I couldn't remember who he was. 'David Poe,' he said. 'Stringer. We met last week in the court session.'

'Oh,' I said. 'What have they sent you for? I would have thought all the nationals would have sent their crime boys.'

I said this in loud, ringingly dismissive tones, in the hope that one or two of the passing big shots might overhear.

'They sent me anyway, seeing as I'm familiar with the local area.'

So now he was an expert. He had probably looked through a few back copies of the *Record* to find out my name. Thanks to his previous visit, he would be able to stand in the pub with the other guys and say things like, 'Independence was taken very seriously round here, you know' and 'The thing about this area is . . .'

And I was supposed to help him out. I was going to be his source for those all-important insider titbits that might pull his story forward from page eleven to page five – his bit of local colour.

You can get stuffed, pal, I thought venomously. If I'd wanted to hang out with jerks like you I'd have moved to London years ago.

The Big Boys had all leapt into their cars and were screeching off to drive back to hotels and guest houses mostly ten minutes' walk away. David Poe followed me as I walked up Church Street.

'Whereas actually,' he was saying, 'I'm completely ignorant.'

Honesty is just one more technique as far as some people are concerned. I didn't reply.

'And – this won't really surprise you – I need your help.'

'There isn't anything you can't work out on your own,' I said, walking briskly.

He trotted next to me. 'You could show me round, if you have time that is . . .'

'No, I don't have time. I work for a living. This is not the only story happening round here just because it's the only one you're interested in.'

'You could give me a few pointers . . .'

'If I have any leads I'll be following them up myself.'

45

'I could shadow you.'

'No. Absolutely not. Forget it.'

We walked along in silence for a while. I was beginning to feel less harsh than I sounded. At least he had come straight to the point – at least he hadn't pretended that he wanted to take me out to dinner.

'Dinner?' he said.

I turned to face him. 'Get your notebook out,' I said. He looked at me, then he stuck his hand in the pocket of his over-sized jacket and pulled out a hand-held tape recorder. He held it up in his hand. 'If you want a nice walk,' I said, 'go up to Rutland Water, it's a big puddle on the way to Stamford. They have watersports and a Butterfly Centre. If you want decent fish 'n' chips you have several options but I can recommend Mill Street. Nearest cinema is Melton Mowbray, ten miles away. Try a pork pie while you're at it. Nearest large hospital is Leicester, twenty miles away, so try not to stub your toe.' I leant forward towards the tape recorder. 'Now sod off.'

I turned sharply down Church Passage.

I couldn't resist glancing back at him. He was looking at me, and smiling.

Horseshoes are considered to be a symbol of good luck worldwide. In Russia, they put one by the door. In the States, all over Europe and, I understand, some parts of Syria, they are also associated with good fortune. In America, most people hang them in a downward position. It is only in funny old Britain that we think we have to place them upwards, otherwise the luck will run out.

Except in Rutland, of course. In Rutland, we hang them downwards. Most people round here would think this is terribly quirky and English – their hair would stand on end if you told them it actually makes us more like Europe.

I don't believe in luck, but there is a horseshoe nailed to the front door of my cottage which dates back to the nineteenth century. It is hung the Rutland way, pointing downwards, and every time I notice it I think, nobody can spend their life just waiting for something nice to happen to them. We all have to shape our own destinies.

I believe in electricity – and I believed the quotation which an Uppingham electrician had pushed through my door while I was out that Tuesday. The whole cottage needed re-wiring. It was going to cost me over two thousand pounds.

I had been putting off the re-wiring for years. It needed doing as soon as I moved in – I still only have one power point in each room with cracked plastic surrounds which are almost falling off the walls. It's amazing I haven't electrocuted myself before now. I had been planning to get it done straight away – I can't decorate properly until I do – but it cost me a fortune to get the stairs put in. When I moved in, you reached the two tiny rooms upstairs by a wooden ladder. I sleep on a futon because there is still no way you could get a bed up there.

I didn't have two thousand pounds. My mortgage was taking every penny of my measly salary. I had only been able to buy the cottage in the first place with the minimum deposit – and I'd only scraped that together because our gran left us a bit of money and I'd lived at home for five years after school, moonlighting in a pub three nights a week.

I sat at my kitchen table and held the quote in my lap, pulling faces. I had been there for over three years and it still needed all sorts of renovation. I had got my mortgage on the condition that the remedial works were done, and I was way behind. I was sick of worrying about money.

I hate people who tap at windows.

I was sitting glumly at my kitchen table, staring at the electrician's quote and trying to summon up the energy to make myself a sandwich and a cup of tea. The tapping was not that loud but its source was so unexpected that I jumped anyway.

Miss Crabbe could have knocked at my door but she probably knew I wouldn't answer. She must have seen me pulling up outside and thought she would catch me before I ran a bath. When I looked up from the table, I could see her shadowed, angular face at the kitchen window. She was looking right at me and her expression was anxious. It was dark outside.

It had been a long day. Doug wanted to add another four pages to the newspaper so that we could do special reports on the murder, which was all well and good but it meant we still had to fill the rest – and if we got another front four that meant there was an extra back four as well. We had brought forward every ad in the basket and the subs were going bonkers. Then, mid-afternoon, I had the inspired idea of running the police photofit slap bang in the middle of the front page, right under WHERE IS GEMMA?. Doug disagreed. He said people would want more copy. So we had a big to-do about that and finally settled on running it on page three but still as big as I wanted. I could write surrounding copy. The only problem was, the police were not giving any details about their source. It might or might not be somebody who lived in the village. Left to my own devices I might have been able to track them down but the gits from the nationals had knocked on every door in Nether Bowston over the weekend. Nobody would talk. It was all right for them. As soon as somebody was charged and the whole thing became *sub judice*, they would disappear back to London. I still had to live round here and do a job of work round here. They were fouling my turf.

So I was not in the best of moods as I rose from my kitchen chair. Miss Crabbe had disappeared from the window and re-appeared at my door. My front door opens straight onto my sitting room, so when you open it, you feel you have already invited someone in.

'I suppose you've heard?' she said, making her way through to the kitchen. 'About the man. Sounded like one of those down-and-out types to me. Probably homeless. Do you think he's still around? I know they are supposed to be searching the barns.'

'I think that's highly unlikely,' I said wearily. Miss Crabbe's first name is Emily but I have never been able to bring myself to call her that. Emily is a little girl's name. Calling her 'Miss Crabbe' would seem too formal, considering how long we have been neighbours. So I call her nothing.

'The police were round here this morning, doing house-to-house. That's what they call it, isn't it?'

God, she's a pain, I thought. 'Yes.'

'They couldn't give me much of a description, though. Dark curly hair. Do you think he had a bit of colour in him and they don't like to say? Are they allowed to say these days?'

'They are allowed to say. He wasn't black. They told us. They were supposed to send us a photofit.' How could I get this tiresome woman out of my house? 'I don't think he's still around. They were talking about seeing him in a car. If he's abducted Gemma, it's not very likely, is it?'

'Unless he's murdered her too and they just haven't found her yet. God, she could be buried just a few feet from here, within earshot.' Miss Crabbe had a fertile if illogical sense of imagination.

I had a bright idea. 'Are you worried? Do you want me to come and check your doors and windows?' Twenty minutes at her place, then I could come home and have my bath.

She hesitated. 'No, I'm not nervous. But you could come and have an omelette if you like. I was just about to do one for myself. It's no trouble.'

Miss Crabbe's chatter was a high price to pay for supper – but I had had one of her omelettes before and it had been delicious. I was starving.

*   *   *

The outer shells of our homes may have been similar but from the inside you would not have believed that Miss Crabbe and I inhabited the same architectural space. Our cottages are semis, but hers was renovated in the seventies. Her kitchen had been moved to the back and the rest of the downstairs interior gutted and made open-plan, with a gallery area instead of the front upstairs box room. She had had it all shelved in plywood with a teak finish. Her sitting room was teak as well, with round brass handles on all the cupboard doors.

And all over the place, there were books; detective books, romances, Ancient Greek history, you name it. A pile of newspapers sat by the settee, so tall it almost reached the top of the arm, and tatty edges hung down where she had taken cuttings and left shreds of paper hanging out. A pair of scissors lay on a grubby, tufted rug with articles strewn around it. I thought that old ladies who lived alone were supposed to be incredibly clean and tidy and dust their vases every day. Not Miss Crabbe. There must have been money behind her somewhere, a small inheritance perhaps. She certainly didn't live off what we paid her at the *Record*. The Village Correspondents get tuppence a line.

She saw me glancing at the detritus. 'A little research of my own,' she said over her shoulder as she went into the kitchen.

I went and leant against the doorpost, watching her while she moved around. Her kitchen was covered in beige tiling. Each tile was decorated by a tiny fern in the bottom left-hand corner, in a slighter darker shade of beige. It was the kind of tiling which anyone with any taste would take personally: I couldn't help looking at those tiles and thinking, they're doing it to get at me.

For someone who was getting on a bit, Miss Crabbe was surprisingly lithe. She bent down to retrieve a glass mixing bowl from a floor cupboard, then raised her arm to pick a carton of eggs from a high shelf. There was a casualness to her gestures. 'Two each or three?' she muttered to herself, fingering the eggs. 'Oh, let's go wild and have three.'

'Do you want me to take a look at your windows?' I asked, remembering how I had wangled my free omelette.

'I'm not as green as I'm cabbage-looking,' Miss Crabbe replied, which seemed to settle the matter. There was a short silence while she cracked the eggs.

'Can I do anything?'

'You can get two place-mats from the dresser and put them on the dining table, then you can sit yourself down. This won't take a minute. I want to talk to you about something.'

My fork was scraping the last small wash of melted butter from my plate, when Miss Crabbe brought up what was on her mind. 'Do you think it would be tasteless to write about a murder in this village, now that one has really happened?'

'You mean for the newspaper?' I asked, kissing the brown cotton serviette she had laid out for me.

She looked irritated. 'No, of course not. That's just journalism. I'm not talking about that. I'm talking about my book.'

Miss Crabbe, it emerged, was writing a book. Actually, she was writing a novel. She was over halfway through it already. It was set in Nether Bowston, and it was about a snail farmer with a secret in his past who was found dead one summer's afternoon with his livestock crawling all over him.

'Do you know, during the war, our housekeeper's father was killed by beetles?' Miss Crabbe added.

I judged that no response was required.

'We had a house in Chatham,' she continued. 'Our housekeeper's family were in the East End and of course she was terribly worried, and when she got the news her father had died, well, we all thought, bloody Germans. It transpired, however, that he was a famous drunk. They lived in a tenement. You won't remember tenements, they're all gone now. Anyway, he had gone out one night and got very badly drunk and arrived home in such a state that he fell asleep downstairs in front of the fire, with his mouth open. When they found him dead the next morning nobody knew quite what had killed him, so they cut him open.' She popped her last forkful of egg into her mouth. 'His stomach was full of beetles. All those places were infested. The beetles had smelt the beer and climbed in and choked him.'

I swallowed. She looked at me.

'That's what my book is based on. Do you think it's a good idea?'

'The snails did it?' I asked, unable to keep a note of incredulity out of my voice.

'Well, in a way,' she replied. 'But they had help, of course. You can't have a murder story and finish it with a load of molluscs being the guilty party.'

I leant back in my chair. 'It sounds original.'

'The thing is,' she said, blowing her nose on her napkin, 'I'm worried that it's a bit tasteless, now that there really has been a murder round here. I wouldn't want anyone to think that was what had given me the idea.'

'I don't think there's any danger of that,' I said carefully. She shrugged.

I left Miss Crabbe just after eleven, skipping the few feet between our front doors. As I opened my own door, I paused and looked behind me.

The lane was dark, the sky flesh-soft and starless. There was a breeze so faint it was scarcely detectable; a long, slow exhalation from the surrounding countryside.

There was a copper-beech hedge opposite the cottages, untrimmed and clotted with dry brown leaves. It seemed odd to me that the leaves were so dead and crisp at that time of year, when everything else was green and babyish. They rattled lightly, as if the hedge was full of locusts.

I always double-lock my doors and check the bolts, but that night I did it twice. Two people had been killed nearby, just over a week ago.

In my bedroom, I huddled down under the duvet and listened to the comforting clumping of Miss Crabbe walking up and down her teak gallery. Perhaps I should have asked her back here to check *my* windows, I thought. I fell asleep thinking about beetles, aware of the nothingness outside.

I was in work early the following day. Our deadline was approaching. Doug and Cheryl were there already.

The photofit had arrived and was sitting on my desk. I pulled off my coat as I sat down. Cheryl was making me a coffee.

'The quality is really good,' she said, as she approached me, mug in hand. 'Doug thinks we should definitely go with it.'

I was looking down. Cheryl put the coffee on the edge of my desk but I scarcely registered her action, reaching out for it with an automatic hand. I was staring at the photofit, wondering if I was imagining it – but the more I stared the more certain I became. The hair was longer. There was no earring. The nose was a little too big and I didn't know that he owned a pair of loose red trousers – but they were just the sort of thing he would have picked up on his travels. It looked like Andrew, my brother.

4

The English may not always be the best writers in the world, but they are incomparably the best dull writers.

Raymond Chandler
The Simple Art of Murder

M iss Crabbe's favourite was *Have His Carcase*. She would often flick through it in search of inspiration. 'Carcase' was a wonderful word. A lesser writer would have used 'corpse' – but you could always rely on Dorothy to move beyond the expected phrase. That was why, in Miss Crabbe's opinion, she was streets ahead of boring old Agatha Christie. 'Agatha Crispy', Miss Crabbe called her – all that brisk prose.

The discovery of the body was the most important single event in a murder story – far more important than the murder itself, which usually happened off-stage and quite right too. She couldn't stand those modern novelists who went in for graphic garrotting and exploding eyeballs. How tasteless to describe all those horrible things happening to a living person.

A dead person was fair game. You could be as horrible as you liked to the dead – the more horrible the better. It was important to establish from the outset that your victim was a thing, a conundrum.

Harriet put the head down again and felt suddenly sick.
She had written often enough about this kind of corpse,
but meeting the thing in the flesh was quite different.

She had not realised how butcherly the severed vessels would look, and she had not reckoned with the horrid halitus of blood, which steamed to her nostrils under the blazing sun. Her hands were red and wet. She looked down at her dress. That had escaped, thank goodness.

Miss Crabbe learnt something every time she re-read *Have His Carcase*. It was vital, for instance, that your protagonist was shocked. It would be very bad form if they weren't.

'Butcherly' – what a wonderful adjective.

Much as she loved murder, Miss Crabbe had no feelings either way about violence. Real violence was to her – like having a child or eating peanut butter – quite unimaginable.

Like many things with the potential for inspiring fear, it had a tendency to inspire amusement. Occasionally, at the weekend, she would catch a repeat of *Bugs Bunny* or *Tom & Jerry* and would sit roaring at the television. It seemed entirely reasonable that if you hit somebody in the face with an iron, their features would flatten momentarily before springing back. She loved hospital dramas. The build-up to the calamity was best. Who could resist watching the old man cross the street, the schoolboy climb a tree, the mother drive with her toddler strapped safely into the back seat? Somehow, and soon, they would all coincide in the same casualty department. It was pure Sophocles.

Channel Four had recently started running a first-aid series, one of those ten-minutes-because-there's-a-gap-in-the-schedule programmes. Miss Crabbe tuned in religiously. It amazed her how stupid some people could be. Especially mothers. Mothers were the most stupid of all.

One episode was about how to deal with scalds and burns. A mother with a lot of Formica in her kitchen was cooking dinner; pie in the oven, vegetables on the hob. A silly little boy, eight years old or so, rushed into the kitchen and tipped a pan all over himself. Naturally, he began to scream and the mother dialled 999. At this point, a handsome-sounding man began a voiceover: 'Run cold water over him for fifteen minutes' etc. When the paramedics rushed in and asked what had happened, the panicking housewife shouted, 'He scalded himself! The carrots!'

Faced with melodrama such as this, Miss Crabbe had a tendency to become literal-minded. 'It wasn't the carrots,' she murmured at the screen, 'it was the hot water, *actually*.'

To her way of thinking, such mishaps were intimately connected to the intelligence of the recipient. Violence happened to people who, unlike her, did not have the common sense to avoid it.

On Sundays, she was fond of skimming through the colour supplement of her newspaper on the lookout for her favourite advertisement. It featured an elderly woman sprawled helplessly on the sitting room carpet, next to a beige sofa. A telephone sat on a coffee table, a tantalising three feet away. The elderly woman could not reach it. Fortunately, she had a large red button strapped to her wrist. While her face looked sadly up at the distant phone, the finger of her other hand was pressing the button. The caption beneath the picture read, 'Mrs Hope knows help is coming. Would you?'

Week in, week out, the same advertisement appeared, although the picture varied. Sometimes, Mrs Hope would have tumbled down the stairs. Her arms would be splayed and she would appear to be in a coma but she must have managed to press the button before she sank into unconsciousness because she still knew help was coming. On other occasions, she had slipped in the bathroom. It seemed she had been trying to get out of (or into) the bath while wearing a fluffy dressing gown and full make-up.

Miss Crabbe found herself quite addicted to Mrs Hope's exploits and would leaf through the supplement each Sunday while other sections of the paper lay on the coffee table unread. 'Mrs Hope knows help is coming. Would you?' I have a question of my own, Miss Crabbe would think, reaching out a languid hand for her Sunday morning treat, a Bourbon biscuit, 'Why is Mrs Hope so accident-prone?'

Miss Crabbe had first come to Rutland in 1974, just after it had officially lost its county status. Her sister was married to an Edith Weston man who had a job in the cement works at Ketton. Miss Crabbe's sister had lived in Edith Weston since she married, and was bored and lonely. She had persuaded Miss Crabbe to come to the area by sending her a leaflet from the library entitled *Rutland, England's Hidden Secret*. Miss Crabbe had needed no more persuading.

At that time, the guerrilla war waged by local activists was at its height. County signs which said 'Leicestershire' were torn down in the night and 'Rutland' ones re-erected. Ladies handed out leaflets in the market place in Oakham every Wednesday and Saturday with titles like *The Fight Goes On*. Local council meetings were rumoured to be stormy.

Miss Crabbe joined the ladies with the leaflets for a few weeks. It was a good way to make friends, although she was careful not to mention that she had only recently moved into the area. She researched Rutland's history in the local library in order to help write a pamphlet for visitors. It was mentioned in the Domesday Book, she discovered – which seemed very *fin de siècle* – although at that time it was little more than a ditch on the way to Northumbria. It was always being bequeathed to people – queens, dukes, mistresses – as if the county and its people were an expensive lapdog. The Duke of Rutland was often a minor character in historical dramas, a secondary conspirator betrayed by a larger man, although both of them would end up with their heads lopped off. The present Duke lived in the Vale of Belvoir – technically outside Rutland's border – and was threatening to lie down in front of the tractors of an open-cast mining company which had spotted coal beneath the green and pleasant valley. England was a battleground once more.

Miss Crabbe thought it all wonderfully futile and heroic. She had moved from Kent, which was very twentieth century.

She had first moved into her cottage as a tenant. It was originally owned by the inhabitant of the neighbouring cottage, mad Mr Willow. Mr Willow's family had lived in Nether Bowston for generations. Miss Crabbe would pop round once in a while and he would ramble to her as he wandered about the cottage picking things up, then putting them down again. He knew all the old inhabitants of the village and would casually refer to favours done or slights given going back to the previous century. Miss Crabbe's predecessor in the cottage had been a Mrs Goldaming – but Mrs Goldaming's family had been nothing, he said. Her father was a didakoi, from over Peterborough way, who had done well to marry a local girl. When Mrs Goldaming's father first arrived in Nether Bowston he had slept in ditches. He had caught rats with his bare hands, then taken them to the pub and offered to bite them in return for a pint.

Miss Crabbe let slip that *her* father had been a circuit judge. She was thus assured of mad Mr Willow's unrelenting friendship and confidence.

She was sad when he died but cheered up no end upon the discovery that she was a sitting tenant. He had died intestate and had no close relatives, so there was some confusion over what would happen to the properties. The solicitors dealing with it eventually let her buy hers at a snip. Mr Willow's cottage remained empty for over two years while everything was sorted out. Then there was a sudden flurry of potential buyers, mostly smarmy young couples. One had a toddler – horror of horrors. Miss Crabbe spotted them arriving with the estate agent and spent the whole of their visit clumping loudly up and down the gallery and singing at the top of her voice through the party wall.

Miss Akenside had been calm, measured and not over-friendly. The ideal neighbour. It was through her that Miss Crabbe had begun working as a Village Correspondent for the *Record*, a job which she regarded as a useful training ground for higher things. Miss Crabbe had dabbled in fiction throughout her life, even publishing a couple of short stories in *People's Friend*. But murder was her passion. Only through a murder story could you feel the tug and sway of history – a line which connected you to the very greatest of storytellers: Sophocles, Shakespeare, Dorothy L. Sayers. Funny how they all began with *S*.

After her young neighbour had departed that evening, Miss Crabbe put the omelette plates in a plastic bowl in the sink and climbed the stairs to her gallery. The length of the gallery was shelved – the staircase led up to the centre of it and you had then the option to turn right or left. At one end, there was an oxblood leather armchair, roomy enough to sink into on a cold winter's evening. (The gas fire was downstairs but most of the heat ended up in the gallery anyway.) At the other end, there was a roll-top desk which she had bought not long after she had moved in, from an auction house in Oakham. Miss Crabbe knew that there was never any hope that she would be able to keep her notes in order, so a roll-top was the only way to prevent them colonising the entire cottage. She loved rattling it down at the end of a hard evening's work, then rattling it back up again the following day. She felt as she imagined a shopkeeper might feel lifting the grille on his premises each morning. When she settled in her typist's chair and pushed back the lid on her project, she knew she was open for business.

Underneath the desktop were two sets of tiny drawers, one on either side, in which she kept paperclips, treasury tags and sticky labels (the left); and spare staples, pencil stubs and liquorice toffees (the right).

She pulled out a pencil stub and stuck it behind her ear. Then she opened the red envelope wallet which lay on top of the papers in the middle of the desk. She often found it necessary to re-read the beginning of her work, to get herself in the mood before she got on with it. She had done a hundred and fifty pages but the manuscript was still handwritten, in pencil. She would have to pay somebody to type it up when it was finished. She had never learnt to type herself. Her mother had warned her that if she did, that was all she would ever do.

Miss Crabbe removed the pencil stub from behind her ear and held it poised. Sometimes she would find she was chewing it while she was reading – a filthy habit and the main reason she tried to keep the stubs behind her ear. When she felt her tongue grate against a flake of paint, she would stick the pencil back in place, sometimes absentmindedly reaching for another from the drawer and discovering the first one only upon retiring, as she brushed her hair.

'She knew instantly that he was dead.' This was the phrase that echoed in Miss Hartington's head as she regarded Edward Little's motionless body. It resonated so because it was demonstrably untrue. She had not stared at him and thought, oh, he's dead. On the contrary, she had been standing there for fully three minutes before it finally filtered through to her that she was indeed, for the first time in all her eighty-three years, regarding a corpse.

Most people in the village assumed Miss Hartington to be an elderly eccentric. This was an image which she liked to promote. It seemed to her very jolly that being eighty-three enabled her to misbehave in the way that normally only children were allowed to, and for her misbehaviour to be received with the same benignity. Every now and then, she would pad down to the village shop in her slippers, just to see how everybody politely ignored her unconventional footwear.

Edward Little had been an attractive man and death had, as yet, not marred his finely chiselled features. Not for nothing had he featured in a popular magazine's 1937 list of Britain's One Hundred Most Eligible Bachelors. His photo then had shown a slim young man, with an almost feminine elegance, although the eyes betrayed a certain hardness. The war had knocked the edges off him somewhat. Miss Hartington could remember him returning looking greatly aged, although it only became clear over time just how much damage the war had done. He had been expected to marry. His fiancée had been Emily Grace, a shy but forthright girl from a good family in Cambridgeshire. She had joined the Land Army the instant war had been declared and was later killed by an awful accident involving a tractor while Edward was serving in Egypt. Friends said he had never got over the shock.

He had returned to the family seat but found management of the estate difficult. The old structures had broken down. It was impossible to get staff and he was forced to sell land to survive. It was not for several years that he hit upon the idea of snail farming.

It was one of his livestock which betrayed his current state of mortis to Miss Hartington, as she stood in his paddock that Sunday afternoon, with the bells for evensong beginning to toll in the distance. At first glance, Edward Little looked asleep. His eyes were closed, unusually for a corpse, although his mouth hung open slightly. His arms were slack by his side. He was wearing a worn Norfolk jacket and in a sitting position, leaning against a tree trunk as if he had sat down by it for a rest on the mellow grass and simply dozed off. To his left were the snail hutches, and Miss Hartington's subconscious registered dimly that the wire mesh doors were open. She had only just noticed the dark shapes in the grass and their attendant silvery trails when she saw the irrefutable evidence that Mr Little had departed this world.

In the corner of his half-open mouth, something was moving. Miss Hartington leant forward to see, unwilling to step closer. Many a woman her age would have required glasses at this juncture, but thankfully her eyesight was still excellent.

There was a small, glistening shape. It was a tiny head. Two tiny black tentacles protruded from it, and they were waving from side to side like antennae, as if the horrid little creature was deciding where next to go. The eyes of a snail were located at the base of the tentacles, Miss Hartington knew, although it always looked to her as though they were in the roaming globules at the tip. They had extremely sharp tongues, sharp enough to saw their way through large amounts of vegetation. Edward Little had often been seen returning from market with crates full of lettuces past their best. They also ate dead animals.

Edward Little had specialised in Mystery snails. He had shown her one once, holding up a rare albino on the palm of his hand and saying that its favourite food was old spinach. He had heard of a farm in Scotland which had managed to grow a Mystery as big as a tennis ball.

Then, as Miss Hartington stared at the gastropod protruding from Edward Little's mouth, his cheek began to bulge and undulate, as if he were still alive and his tongue were working, trying to extract something stuck fast in a molar, perhaps.

*As she watched with mounting disgust, another glis-
tening head and pair of horns emerged from underneath
his upper lip. The head seemed to swing her way and
move from side to side, as if in greeting.*
Miss Hartington let out an involuntary gasp.

Miss Crabbe stopped and put down her manuscript. There
had been a sound from next door, a sound so slight that it
was already a memory. She did not even know what sort of
sound it had been.

She sighed. The character of Miss Hartington was proving
a little difficult. Her protagonist was, at heart, a somewhat
timid lady, yet she must be endowed with a few eccentricities.
How else would it be credible that she should track down a
killer and bring him or her to justice? There was also the
matter of the all-important twist at the end. You had to have
a twist. It was *de rigueur*.

For some months now, it had been sneaking up on Miss
Crabbe. She knew what had to happen. The question was,
could she bring it off? The trick to managing a surprise
was that it should be entirely inevitable. The Ancients had
it right. You knew from the word go that it was Oedipus at
the place where three roads meet and that the shepherd was
going to give the game away – but it was as if the brain was
happy to be divided into two. It wasn't simply a question
of watching Oedipus writhe around in self-delusion, like an
insect in a jar. You had to share that delusion for it to be
effective, even though you knew exactly what was going to
happen.

The trick, Miss Crabbe felt certain, was to disbelieve in
good and evil. The surprise ending of her book had to lie in
the character of the seemingly ordinary and conventional Miss
Hartington, the detective herself. A murder story was only
interesting if there was some ambiguity, after all. There was
no point in having evil performed by a wholly evil person.

It came again, louder. It was halfway between a moan and a cry – a brief ejaculation of sound which none the less had depth and meaning: a human noise with animal undertones.

Miss Crabbe rose and tiptoed the length of her gallery to the wall that she shared with Miss Akenside. She knelt on the oxblood leather armchair and put her ear to the wall. Her stiff curls flattened against the wallpaper with a soft, seashell noise. For some time there was nothing. Then it came again – a low, restless moan. Poor dear Alison was at it again.

Miss Crabbe had never really suffered from bad dreams. She had slept the sleep of the dead every night, exactly six and a half hours, for as long as she could remember. Her sister had insomnia and would sit glumly in a chair all day in her kitchen at Edith Weston, sipping coffee to keep her awake and posting chocolate biscuits into her sullen mouth with a hand that hardly seemed attached to the rest of her body. Miss Crabbe found that sort of problem incomprehensible.

Alison's difficulty was different, she felt. There was something unnatural about it. It came in waves – whole nights of moaning sometimes, then the sound of movement around the cottage. Miss Crabbe heard it because she stayed up late working. She often did her best stuff at night.

Miss Crabbe returned to her desk, put down her manuscript and pencil and lowered the roll-top. She wasn't in the mood for work. She had not really been in the mood since the discovery of the Cowpers' bodies. She felt, somehow, as if she was ever so slightly culpable in what had happened to them. She knew this was ridiculous – a psychotic could turn up on your doorstep any time. It could have just as easily been her.

At the same time, she could not escape the feeling that to have a murder occur in the village was all too convenient for her purposes. It would be wonderful publicity, after all.

She had already written the disclaimer to go in the front of her book.

Was it wrong to want to take advantage in this way? It wouldn't make the Cowpers any less dead if she didn't. It wouldn't be any help to them if she set fire to the entire manuscript.

She went downstairs to the kitchen. The shattered eggshells from the omelettes still lay in a pink saucer by the side of the sink. She took the saucer over to her swing-bin and tipped the eggshells in, then saw that the bin was almost full. The nights were warm now. She didn't like sleeping with a full bin in the house. You never knew what might come in to take a look.

She had already locked her back door for the night, so she had to withdraw the old iron bolts and turn the key. Her wheely bin lived in the garden during the week. She lifted the lid and dropped in the swing-bin liner, with its handles firmly tied. As she lowered the lid, she looked over to Alison's garden.

Suddenly, Miss Crabbe went hollow inside, the way she did when she drove too quickly over the hump-backed bridge at the end of the lane.

Alison was standing in her garden. The fence between them was a small brown picket fence, no more than three feet high. Alison was on her side of it but close enough for Miss Crabbe to see her clearly in the light that shone from her kitchen.

She was standing deadly still. She was wearing a long t-shirt which came down below her knees. On the front of the t-shirt was a large teddy bear dressed up as a fireman and carrying a hosepipe. It had an idiotic smile. Her feet were bare. Her short hair, normally neat and straight and modern, was ruffled and spiky. She was staring at Miss Crabbe. It was a stare of open-eyed malevolence.

Miss Crabbe froze, then wondered if she should say something. What did you do with sleepwalkers? Weren't you supposed to guide them gently back to their beds? But Alison wasn't walking anywhere. She was standing stock still, and staring a stare that rooted Miss Crabbe to her back step. She tried to tell herself that she had shared an omelette with this young woman only hours before, but their congenial supper belonged to an ordinary life, a life made up of ordinary days – not the night-time world they now found themselves in, where anything could happen.

Miss Crabbe stepped backwards as soundlessly as possible, back into her well-lit kitchen. She closed the door, turned the key, bolted her bolts. Abandoning her washing up, she turned out the kitchen light and went through to her sitting room, where she stood for a moment. She did not want to go up to her bedroom. It also looked out over the back of the cottage, and she knew she would not be able to resist looking down to see if Alison was still there. She could not bear the thought that she might look up and see her. She did not want to be looked at that way again. It had been a look of pure evil.

5

O Rose, thou art sick!

William Blake
The Sick Rose

I sleepwalk sometimes. I have no memory of it. I only know I do it because of the traces I leave behind; objects moved around the house, doors left open. Sometimes, I notice that my feet are grubby and there is soil or a grass stain on my nightwear, and I know that I have been out in the garden.

It comes and goes. When I was little, it was nearly every night. My brother Andrew and I shared a room. After I had gone to sleep, he would get up and, taking the mattress and blankets from his bunk, bed himself down across the door, so that I couldn't get out of the room. I don't know how old he was when he did this – I only know because he told me about it a couple of years ago. I try and remember it when I get annoyed with him, which is frequently. A small boy slept across my bedroom door, like a guard dog.

I never think of myself as a small girl. I feel as though I have always been grown up.

It was only in adolescence that the sleepwalking became a problem, and only then because I didn't get myself back to bed in time for the morning and would wake up in odd places like behind the settee. My mother had to hunt high and low for me in the mornings, finding me eventually because my feet were sticking out. Common to these episodes seemed to be a desire to burrow, to squeeze myself into the smallest space into which my clumsy thirteen-year-old body would

69

fit. This seems peculiar to me now, as I am something of a claustrophobe.

Soon after, Andrew left home. He had graduated from our local comp with zero qualifications bar woodwork, and took only a rucksack full of clothing and a handful of chisels. We heard nothing for years.

Being at home was very quiet and unpleasant after he left. I was furious. It was all right for him. He was not around to see the hurt he had caused; my mother's perpetually strained expression, my father's bruised silence. I may not be the most dedicated of daughters but I don't think I could have wounded them in the way that Andrew did. They had already lost one child, after all, in an accident too horrible for words.

'Too horrible for words'. Can that be literally true? Can anything be too horrible to bear articulation? It depends on who is doing the articulating, I suppose. For the inarticulate, many things must be too horrible for words – or too awkward or unusual or plain. My father is a man who cannot bring himself to say, 'How are you?' Instead, he looks at you, grunts, then tilts his chin minutely upwards, a tiny gesture of interrogation. In response I say, 'Fine, Dad. You?' He nods.

My mother achieves the same effect by the opposite means. Words spill out of her. She talks as if talking will pre-vent thought – and thought is something which must at all costs be prevented. 'Hello Alison you're looking your usual self, I'm fine apart from my back but I told you all about that, your father went to the chiropodist last week, I made him go, kettle's boiling' is a typical greet-ing.

In response to my mother's verbosity, I become my father. I grunt and nod.

Which came first, I wonder? My mother's talkativeness or my father's silence? Did the one create the other or merely encourage it? Maybe that was what they saw in each other in the first place, two pieces of a jigsaw which could lock together snugly, then merely co-exist.

My baby brother's death is the only thing that has ever happened to my parents which is out of the ordinary, and I wonder sometimes to what extent it has created them. I was five when it happened. It is my earliest memory – I have no idea whether Mum and Dad were any different before. If it is my earliest memory, does that mean that it has also created me? I don't believe in the subconscious. All that buried self is good and buried as far as I'm concerned. Perhaps I sprang to life fully formed at five years old, one April.

The memory goes like this.

I am in my room. It is bedtime. I have a dressing gown on over my nightie. It is made of a squeaky, quilted fabric and there are large roses on it, full-blown roses. I will grow too big for it soon. My forearms will get cold because they protrude from the sleeves.

Our council house is large but each room in it is tiny, as if it is a series of hutches knocked together. The walls are thin. Andrew's room is next to mine and we communicate by tapping with our knuckles on the embossed wallpaper, which has a satiny feel.

Andrew is sitting on the end of my bed. He has sherbet. The sherbet is bright pink and encased in a plastic packet shaped like a tiny, see-through suitcase. You flip a little plastic catch and open the lid, then hold it up to your mouth and lick the sherbet from inside. It prickles on the tongue.

In the shop at the end of the road, there are many different ways of persuading children to eat sherbet; sherbet Fountains, sherbet Dib-dabs – sherbet encased in flying saucers made of rice paper which collapse then explode, making your gums tingle. In my case, persuasion is unnecessary. Sherbet is the most sensory experience I have – the sparkle of it, an almost-pain, magic in the mouth.

Andrew has left me alone for a moment, to get something

from his room. He has left the tiny case of sherbet open on my bed, with strict instructions that I am not to touch it until he returns. I am trying to work out how I can get sherbet into my mouth without touching, prepared to break the spirit but not the letter of the law.

This is something I can remember quite clearly from childhood; the greed, the constant wanting. There was a girl in one of my classes who came from a road called The Crescent. Her mother packed her off to school each day with three biscuits wrapped in greaseproof paper. Myself and other girls used to crowd round her at break time and demand a bite each – a small, aspirational nibble at what it might be like to have a middle-class mother who worried that her child might get peckish between classes. When the girl – Susan, I think – finally put her foot down and refused, we crowded round her anyway, watching her. I remember whispering, 'We never liked your stupid biscuits you know. They taste like poison.'

Suddenly, the door to my bedroom flies open and my mother storms in. We have been caught. She grabs one of my upper arms and hauls me to my feet. I give a small cry.

As she pushes me down the stairs, she is muttering. I can't hear what she is saying.

My brother is in the sitting room. His face is blank. I know that this means we are in serious trouble.

My mother prods me with the ends of her fingers and I go and clamber onto the settee, next to my brother.

I am expecting a tirade, but instead, my mother begins to pace the room, still muttering. Perhaps she is trying to decide how badly we are to be punished. I sneak a glance at Andrew to see if he can give me a clue but he is staring straight ahead. It is not like him to be so unhelpful.

I don't know how long we sit there but it feels like for ever.

Suddenly, my mother turns. She falls on her knees on the

carpet in front of us, grabs at us with her large hands and pulls us down. I assume the kneeling position I have learnt in school assembly, sitting back on my heels, head low, palms pressed together. It is quite different from the one we use in church each Sunday, where I kneel upright and hold on to the wooden shelf attached to the pew in front.

My mother entwines her fingers. Grown-ups do that when they pray.

My mother is saying something like, 'These children are wicked, Lord. They are wicked to the core. Show me how to knock the wickedness out of them, so that they may be spared Your wrath. Do not strike them down, O Lord. Show me how to improve them.'

I pray for forgiveness and promise that I will never eat sherbet again.

After a while, her voice becomes a mutter. I lift my head and creak my eyelids open, peering through trembling lashes. My mother's eyes are tight closed. I sneak a look at Andrew but he is kneeling next to me and I can't see him properly without turning, which would be risky.

We pray until my knees begin to ache.

Then there is a noise from the room above us, a sort of *whumphing*, like air falling at speed. At the same time, there is a crack and tinkle of breaking glass.

The room above us belongs to Baby James. Baby James arrived not long after Christmas. The Baby, we had been warned in advance, was going to use up all the money, so that was why there were no big presents.

Andrew and I have recovered from our resentment remarkably quickly. We have realised that Baby James is a good thing because our mother spends her days trying to stop him crying and has, until tonight, been much more lax with us. We feel well-behaved in comparison with Baby James. At least we don't scream all the time.

All three of us lift our heads. The sound is so unusual that

Andrew and I forget to be afraid. Our mother clambers to her feet and rushes out of the room.

There is a pause. Through the open sitting-room door, we can see her shadow in the hallway.

Then she begins to scream.

As we run out into the hall, we collide with her running back in to get us. She pushes us towards the front door. As she opens it, a flood of freezing air rushes in. There is another bang from upstairs.

Out in the street, people arrive. I can hardly see them in the dark. My mother has stopped screaming and is moaning and gasping for breath. Somebody holds her arms. Men rush past us into the house. There is the distant, insistent clamour of a siren.

The fire engine is as big as a dragon. It belches and coughs. We are pushed to one side. My feet are bare. I tread on something sharp, and begin to cry. Somebody big and strange picks me up and holds me. My feet sting. I try and twist my head to look back at our house but all I can see is darkness and people. There is shouting. The person holding me turns and begins to walk down the street, away.

That night, Andrew and I are put to bed in somebody's lounge, on wobbly camping beds which have been blown up with a foot pump. Our father comes in and stands in the doorway. 'Where's Mum?' I ask.

'In hospital,' he says. 'But she'll be back tomorrow.'

We were never told exactly how Baby James had died. I remember watching a documentary, many years later, about how dangerous cheap furnishings were. It made it sound as though any council house could burst into flames sponta-neously and fill with poisonous fumes in seconds. I remember walking round our new house – we had been rehoused on an estate a mile away from our old home – and thinking, could this one burn as well? Could this one fill with poison?

If our mother had not been downstairs chastising Andrew and me, maybe she would have noticed the fire earlier, maybe the baby could have been saved. I wondered sometimes if she blamed us, blamed our wickedness. I haven't a clue – neither she nor my father has ever discussed it with us. *Too horrible for words.*

Andrew asked me about it once.

I was ten, I think. We were in the sitting room, watching television. It was a Saturday morning. Our parents were out.

'Alison, do you remember the fire?'

At that age I was still going to church with my mother and my faith had temporarily acquired something of her fervour. I loved the routine, the ritual. I wanted some prettiness in my life, some colour and gleaming. I sometimes think that half the membership of High Churches like ours can be attributed to stained glass.

I glanced over at Andrew, surprised at his question, the lightness of it. I said something like 'It was God's will. He wanted the baby to be with him.'

Andrew looked at me. He never went to church.

He rose from the settee and went and sat against the wall, drawing up his knees and wrapping his arms round them. How old would he have been? Twelve, thirteen?

I thought he was crying, so I went over to him and put a hand on his arm, but when he lifted his face, it was dry. He looked at me with dull misery.

'I thought I could rely on you,' he said. 'You're the only one left.'

He never asked me again.

I sometimes wondered about asking my mother, on Sunday mornings as we walked over to All Saints. She always strode at such a fierce pace. We walked more slowly on the way back but talking then would have seemed frivolous, somehow. I was growing almost as tall as her, tall enough to borrow her old coats. She always wore a headscarf. She had a whole collection, fine ones made of slippery silks with tangled leafy patterns.

Around the age of twelve I discovered nail varnish and stopped going to church. There was a month or so of rows, then she gave up. Andrew's disappearance put the lid on it, really, her disappointment in her children, our wicked, wicked ways.

By the time he left home, I was already planning my own escape. I knew exactly what I wanted to replace the stained glass. I wanted a garden. I didn't much care what the garden was attached to as long as it was out of town, near fields. I wanted silence. I wanted to be away from the sight of my large mother on her hands and knees, at prayer, scrubbing floors – away from my small father shrunk into an armchair watching whatever channel the television had been left tuned to because he couldn't be bothered to get up and change it. They must have been the last people in the country to get a remote control.

I wanted a short drive after work, through open country-side, to a place where I could sit alone.

I don't visit them much now. Living a few miles up the road is a good excuse for not visiting them. My proximity proves that I don't need to get away from them, so I don't feel obliged to turn up every Sunday clutching a pot plant. Neither of them can drive, so there isn't any danger they would ever visit me. Mum has never learnt, and Dad lost his licence years ago after one too many pints of County.

Because I can drop in any time, I hardly ever do. This seems to suit them as well as it suits me. Never once, on Andrew's occasional visits to me, has he ever called in on Mum or Dad. I know better than to suggest it.

I suppose that irritation with your parents can reach such a pitch that you feel obliged to put a bit of geographical distance between you and them. I had one schoolfriend who claimed she was emigrating to New Zealand because she couldn't stand the way her father said, 'So, d'you like grapefruit, then?' every time she ate one. But is it possible for irritation to reach such an extreme pitch that it becomes hatred? Can a minor emotion multiplied to the nth degree become a major one? I have always thought of such extremity as so *other* that it would never apply to me – but perhaps that says something about the difference between Andrew and me.

I asked him, once, why he left home so young and he said, 'I couldn't have stayed as long as you did. I'd have killed them. I'm not like you.'

I am not sure where Andrew lives now and I don't think he's that sure either. He is loosely based in London, which means he keeps a bag of clothes and his tool kit at a friend's house. Sometimes I ring and the friend says, 'He's been in India for two months. I think he went for carvings.' A month or so later, Andrew turns up on my doorstep with a little weeping god in his pocket and says, 'Paul said you'd rung.' He will have come back to England with a whole rucksack full of weeping gods which he will have sold at Greenwich market to make back some of his air fare. In between, he does a bit of carpentry or painting and decorating. Every now and then, he does a few drugs. He went through a heroin phase a few years back. When I told him off about it he said, 'Oh relax, for God's sake. I smoke it.'

Sometimes, I see Andrew with other people's eyes. He is shorter than me, with a twisted wire of muscle that leads up one arm, across the shoulders, and down the other. He keeps his hair so short it isn't hair. He wears an earring in one ear and has fat hands. There is a bullishness about him, particularly when he feels insecure.

I am not surprised that whoever spotted him lurking around Nether Bowston informed the police.

*　　*　　*

Nether Bowston, like most of the villages, has a variety of local nicknames. Bottom Bowston, The Bottom, Nether Bagwash. At school, there was a Geography teacher who was a big fan of Lou Reed and The Velvet Underground. He would talk about the band during lessons and one day one of the boys said, 'Mr Taylor, can you stop going on about those Vampire Underpants.' We all giggled, and the teacher never mentioned them again. If you mis-name something, you are stating your superiority, especially if it cannot mis-name you back. You are making things, or people, into something they are not, changing them in the eyes of the world.

It is the same with twinning, I suppose. The village of Whitwell is twinned with Paris – they have the official sign as you enter – and this is as much a joke against Paris as against Whitwell. Many Rutland villages are twinned with each other, if only in name; Great and Little Casterton; Whissendine in the north-west corner of the county and Essendine in the east; North and South Luffenham.

Nether Bowston once had an Upper Bowston a mile or so away, but that is now no more than two derelict cottages not far from where I live. It was in one of these cottages that I found my brother.

Andrew had camped out in the cottages before. He turned up one Friday night just after I had left to spend the weekend with Joey and Linda, my friends in Birmingham. I only found out about it six months later, on his following visit. He doesn't normally stick around if he can't find me. I offered him a key to my place once, but he said, 'I'll only lose it.'

It was lunchtime. I didn't have much time to spare. I had left the office pretending that I had to re-visit the Cowper house for my copy and Doug was not pleased. We were only a day away from our deadline.

Andrew was lying behind one of the cottages, in the sun. He was leaning back against a large woven bag that he had bought in Guatemala, multicoloured hieroglyphs against a black background. Next to him, on the scrubby grass, were his tobacco tin, his matches, a bottle of Evian water and a battered paperback of a novel by some Russian I had never heard of. His eyes were closed.

'You've grown your hair,' I said. I wouldn't have called his curls black myself, more earthy brown.

He opened his eyes, then closed them again. 'I wasn't expecting you until this evening,' he said. 'I've only just got here.'

I took off my coat and dropped it beside him, then sat down. 'I thought I'd better come and find you before the police did,' I said. 'They're all over the place. I'm surprised you haven't been picked up. Roll me a fag.'

He levered himself upright, using both elbows, took a swig from his water bottle then passed it over to me. He rubbed his face with one hand and fiddled in his pockets for his Rizlas.

'I don't have much time,' I said. 'I'm supposed to be at the office.'

He didn't reply. Andrew has always despised my need to hurry, and I have always despised the way he despises it. It is easy to be cool when you don't have a mortgage – that's why Andrew has never got one. It wouldn't go well with his street cred.

'Why the police?' he asked as he licked the paper. 'What have I done this time?'

'God,' I said, 'don't you ever read any papers?'

'Nope. Specially not that community-service rag you work for.'

I took the cigarette from him impatiently and picked up the box of matches lying beside the tobacco tin. 'You've got to go and eliminate yourself from inquiries,' I said in low, dramatic tones, then lit the cigarette.

'Inquiries into what?' He was rolling another fag but he stopped and lay back on his bag, closing his eyes.

'Andrew, this isn't funny. There's been a murder.'

Even Andrew sat up at that one. 'Where?'

'Just round the corner from here. Some people called Cowper. Two of them. The daughter's missing. It was only a week ago.'

'Bloody hell, Alison,' he said roughly, protectively, and I felt a sudden rush of affection for him.

'Somebody saw you around here,' I said, then coughed. A small shred of tobacco had got caught in my throat as I inhaled.

'I came by. It was a Sunday but you weren't in. So I went to Nottingham to see a girl. She's Swedish. We met in Germany.'

'I thought you wouldn't be out here all week.' I got to my feet. 'We'd better ring the police. You can do it from my place. I hope this Swedish bird is going to give you an alibi.'

'No probs. She's solid.'

I got to my feet and brushed dead grass off my leggings. 'You've got to come now. I'm in enough trouble already. Are you driving a car these days? There was another sighting of a man in a car.'

He gave me a lingering, despairing look. Andrew was no more likely to buy a car than he was to get a job as an estate agent and settle down in Kettering.

'Well,' I said, turning to go, 'you'd better start trying to remember the details of the drivers who gave you lifts to Nottingham.'

We walked back to the cottage and I left him there, extracting a promise that he would ring Inspector Collins immediately, then take a look at my bathroom shelves, which were wobbly.

It was only as I was driving back to Oakham that I realised what Andrew's appearance on the scene of our murder meant. The photofit would be withdrawn. We were going to have to redesign page three.

*　　*　　*

Cheryl wasn't in our office, so I went up the stairs to Doug's, from where I could hear conspiratorial voices.

Doug was sitting behind his desk with his feet up on a pile of boxes. There was a heap of page proofs in front of him – his jam jar full of worn pencils sat on top of it. In the corner was the staff Christmas tree, a plastic one which could be collapsed and leant against a wall. It lived in Doug's office all year round, until it was time to take it down to Reception.

Doug was leaning back in his chair and his head was tipped backwards, exposing his fleshy neck. Cheryl was standing behind him and massaging his temples, just below the hairline of fine white fluff which feathered his speckled scalp. Cheryl was not thin herself. Gold bangles tinkled gently on her plump wrists with the rounded motion of her fingers. She looked up as I came in.

'Our editor has decided he's having a bad day,' she said gently.

'Oh dear,' I said, standing in the doorway. 'I'm about to make it worse.'

Doug opened his eyes and sat up quickly, lowering his legs. Cheryl folded her arms and sighed in soft despair.

'What?' Doug asked.

I leaned against his doorpost. 'The photofit is about to be eliminated. We're going to have to drop it. Andrew was in Nether Bowston last weekend. It was him.'

Doug groaned, leaning forward and putting the heels of both hands against his eyes, rubbing at them. Then he sat up and beamed.

I looked at Cheryl.

'He's cracking up,' she said.

'Take a look at the nationals,' Doug said cheerfully. 'They must have got it last night. They all ran with it today.'

A heap of papers was sitting crossways on a chair by his door. I bent and picked them up.

'Take them downstairs,' Cheryl said to me, placing both hands on Doug's shoulders and levering him back into his chair. 'I'll be down in ten minutes.'

Doug said, 'We can't do this now.'

As I made my way down the stairs, Cheryl was replying. 'Shut up, you old fool.'

It was a slow week for news and the tabloids were still going big on the Cowpers' case, most running with the death-in-rural-idyll angle. They had all used the photofit, and I thought how much it would amuse Andrew that he had made it into every national newspaper while I still worked for the *Record*. I scanned the coverage for David Poe's by-line but couldn't see anything accredited to him or the Press Agency. One paper had run a picture of our village green, a tiny triangle of grass with a stone war memorial and a set of ancient wooden stocks. They had persuaded Mr Walters from Rye Street to stand next to the memorial and look up at it sadly. The caption said, 'Village in shock'.

Sarah from advertising was leaving some proofs on Cheryl's desk. 'You might as well give those to me,' I said.

She came over and stood next to me, looking down at what I was reading. Several of the papers had run a photo of Gemma in a school blazer, looking much younger than seventeen, I thought. Her hair was long and parted on one side, held back by two plastic clips, as if her brown locks were a stage curtain only partially lifted from the quiet drama of her face. Her eyebrows were heavy, but her other features small. It was an unformed face, I thought.

'They were in here while you were out, some of that lot,' Sarah said, nodding at the papers, 'trying to be all chummy – you know how they are.'

'Do you think she did it?' I said, gazing at Gemma's photo.

'Looks like it, doesn't it?' Sarah said quietly. 'I should think she's long gone by now.'

*   *   *

82

It was dark by the time I got home. I was tired but we had worked hard and done the bulk of the next day's work. It was probably going to be an easier deadline day than most, ironically. Doug was weighing in, sleeves rolled up, and his enthusiasm was catching. The adrenalin of recent events had affected us all.

I half expected that Andrew would have hopped it, leaving the key on the kitchen table and the cottage unlocked – he'd done it before – but a light was on as I parked my car on the verge.

Andrew had his feet up on my saggy two-seater sofa and was forking his way through a Pot Noodle. I keep a small supply for emergencies. His gaze was fastened upon my television, which blared an American soap. 'This is brilliant,' he said as I came in, without looking up. I wasn't sure whether he meant the soap or the noodles. Andrew spends so much of his life being organic that when he comes to my place he likes to gorge himself on as much consumerism as he can lay his hands on.

'How were the police?' I asked above the television. 'Can you turn that down?'

He put down the Pot Noodle and picked up the remote. 'The old biddy from next door was complaining.'

'It's not a very thick wall. So how was it?'

'It took bloody hours,' he muttered, finally wrenching his gaze away from the television. 'They asked me to stick around.'

'What do you expect?' I asked, turning. 'It is a murder inquiry.'

He followed me into the kitchen.

'Those shelves in the bathroom are desperate. I suppose you put them up yourself. Your loo's leaking again and I tightened the screws on all your kitchen cupboard doors. But do you want the really bad news?'

I took the kettle to the sink. 'No.'

'Your roof. The timbers are worse. I think you're going to have to sue your surveyors.'

I stopped and looked at him. 'You're *joking*.'

'This cottage is a disaster,' he added, unhelpfully. 'I can't believe you bought a place without consulting me.'

We have been through this one before. 'You were in Pakistan, I believe.'

'Mind your foot!' he said suddenly.

I had just turned from the sink. I stopped, kettle in hand, and looked down.

There was a tiny corpse at my feet.

It was a mouse, splayed out on its back as neatly as if on a dissecting slab. Its limbs were spread and its stomach ripped open. A miniature mess of purple and pink intestine had tumbled onto my lino.

'Oh, for God's sake,' I said, putting down the kettle. 'Did you leave the doors open this afternoon?'

'Your walls are damp, that's why you get so much mildew. You should leave the doors open as much as you can. It's a present, you know. Cats leave them as presents for humans; they think you'll be pleased.'

I was not pleased. 'You might have cleared it up,' I snapped, reaching under the sink for a dustpan.

Andrew clearly thought his next remark very funny. 'I thought I should wait until you came home and drew a chalk line round it.'

Twenty minutes later, Andrew remembered the note. It was in his pocket. It had been delivered an hour after the police had left. It was on lined paper torn from an exercise book and folded into a very small square. It had been pushed through the letterbox even though the door was open. There had been no knock.

Dear Alison
Can you come and see me somtime as soon as you

can. We are not on the phone anymore, but you can remember our place its by the electricity pilons.

Tim

I went to see Tim Gordon the following day, although I couldn't get there until we had put the paper to bed.

It was early evening and the birds in the trees were going bananas, tweeting like old ladies queuing for their pensions. Now that it was too late, the sun had come out. The evening was cold and golden.

It must have been over fifteen years since I had last visited him. I used to cycle up from Oakham on a Sunday afternoon, to play in his father's junk yard. Technically speaking, I suppose he was my first boyfriend. It wasn't remotely physical but there was a certain intensity to our friendship based, perhaps, on a shared unhappiness with the rest of our lives. It coincided with my religious phase. I knew he was beneath me, but being kind to him reinforced my belief in myself, as if I would have to be pure of heart and mind to be nice to a boy like him when there was so little in it for me.

His family lived in a row of council houses on the far side of the village, on the way to the industrial estate. Most villages in Rutland have that sort of housing tucked discreetly out of sight; modern semis made of a dun-coloured brick which is supposed to blend with the local stone but usually ends up looking just muddy. It is in those houses that the countryside's true inheritors live, the grandchildren and great-grandchildren of the farm workers and servants who worked on the big estates. None of them would dream of living in a period cottage like mine.

Tim was an only child who lived with his parents in the last house in the village, a bald semi with no exterior decoration but a forest of rusting cars out back. I went straight round the outside of the house, like I used to, and noticed that the

85

wooden lattices on the side of it were empty. I wondered if they always had been. I thought, when I was a child, he and I had the same sort of life.

As I rounded the house, I saw him at the back of the yard. The metal hulks around him had mostly lost their headlights and looked eyeless, malicious. He was bent into the bonnet of one. It looked as though the car was eating him.

Hearing my steps, he straightened. His face was red and he was holding a cloth. He nodded, then came towards me.

It is always a surprise when people you have known since childhood turn out to be particularly tall or fat. Tim Gordon had turned out both. He was well over six foot, large enough for his plump, moonish face to tip down towards you as he spoke. His chest described a waterfall, an uninterrupted curve plunging from his chin. He always seemed to be leaning forward a little too far, a trait which was noted by the tough lads at our comprehensive school who followed him around chorusing, 'Tim-*ber*!' It didn't appear to upset him. He seemed to enjoy the attention.

He stood holding the oiling cloth, passing it from hand to hand, and refused to look at me. His gaze appeared to be fixed somewhere to the left of my shoulder.

It occurred to me, all at once, that it was not beyond the realms of possibility that Tim Gordon was capable of killing someone. Physically, he fitted a certain sort of brief, a hardy perennial of the TV murder story, The Simpleton Who Didn't Really Mean It. How many people do really mean it? If most murders are impulsive, maybe anyone who has impulses is capable of it.

Tim stopped pretending to wipe his hands and, still without looking at me, said, 'Hello. Nice of you to come. I know you're busy.'

I searched his face for clues. 'How are you, Tim? What is it?'

'Can we go somewhere?' he said. 'Mum and Dad . . .'

As we walked back to my car, I tried to picture myself dead, my throat cut, or strangled perhaps, lying underneath some undergrowth in nearby woodland. I tried to imagine fear, but fear is unimaginable. You feel fear, not imagine it.

Is this how it happens? I thought. Do people do stupid things, walk into stupid situations, because of a lack of imagination?

As we passed the side of the house, I glimpsed the dim figure of Mrs Gordon, moving past a frosted kitchen window.

'Where do you want to go?' I asked, as I unlocked the passenger door for him, and he waved a large arm in the air. 'Do you want a drink?' I said, as I shuffled myself into the driver's seat and reached for my seatbelt. He shook his head.

We drove until we came to a lay-by. The road was deserted. On either side were open fields.

I pulled into the lay-by and turned off the engine. The handbrake creaked. 'Here do you?' I asked, sitting back in my seat and making it very clear that it did me.

He nodded. I noticed his gaze flick towards a half-consumed packet of mints in the plastic well in front of the gearstick, wrapper spiralling haphazardly. I picked them up and offered him one but he refused, so I took one myself.

'I know I ought to go to the police,' he said hesitantly.

The story of a lifetime unfolded before me. DOUBLE KILLER CONFESSES TO OUR GIRL.

'I know I should've done,' he continued, 'but it was mainly Mum and Dad. Well, you know, I like to look after them and it would've given them a real fright. So I sort of kidded myself it wasn't her. I knew it was, but I kidded myself. I thought it was just maybe a girl or someone. She didn't look much like the picture in the paper. But I know it was.'

I sat. I did not even dare to chew my mint, which was

jammed in an uncomfortable lump against the roof of my mouth.

'So then I thought, I'll go see Alison, and she'll tell me. Maybe you could go to the police with me. Or tell me who I've got to ring to go with me, if I need anyone that is. I don't think I do. Was that okay?'

I made a gesture which was an awkward combination of a shake of the head and a shrug.

'Anyway, I feel a bit bad. I don't know whether it's too late now, whether they'll still be able to find her . . .'

He tailed off and I realised I was supposed to prompt him. The mint was still stuck. My words came out thickly. I tried to think of a phrase which contained no hint of moral censure. 'What happened?' I managed.

He blew air out through his mouth and pulled a face. 'I was driving through Nether Bowston, on my way to Braunston, you know my uncle lives there now?' He looked at me and I nodded, although I had no idea he had an uncle. 'It was the Monday. I'd seen you at the Castle. Well, I'd just got through Bowston, over the humpback, and I was pulling round the corner, and I nearly ran her down. I had to pull over. I wasn't going that fast. She was almost in the middle of the road.' His voice had taken on an anxious tone, as if it was important to convince me he hadn't been speeding. 'I stopped the car and I wound down the window. I was going to tell her to watch it.'

He paused, then frowned. 'She came over, and looked at me. I think I will have a mint.'

I stared at him. He picked up the packet and fiddled with the remaining string of paper. 'You've had these a while, they're all stuck together.' He prised one away and popped it in his mouth.

'She had a weird look on her face, a look like I'd never seen before. Sort of set. She was wearing a coat that was too big for her, somebody else's coat, and she held it wrapped round her as if she was cold, which was pretty odd because it was that warm evening we had. And she said, Will you give me a lift? Where to? I says. Anywhere, she says, Oakham. And then she goes round to the other side and without so much as a by your leave she gets in. I hadn't said yes or anything. And she just sits there without moving. I thought, she's probably ill or something, and I started the car.'

His mint was clearly bothering him as much as mine was bothering me. He gave a gulp and swallowed it whole.

'It's the wrong way for me but by then I was scared of her. So we got to Oakham and I'm glancing over at her saying, where do you want to be dropped off? She hasn't said a word the whole time and I'm just wanting shot of her and I'm looking over and suddenly she says, keep driving, please, just keep driving.'

He paused and sighed. I saw that he was close to tears. His voice dropped and cracked. 'I know I should've pulled over and gone and got someone, I *know* . . . my Dad's going to be disappointed in me because I didn't do what I should've done. I should've, but I kept driving and by then we were down the High Street so I took the Stamford road and we were out and coming up past the reservoir, Rutland Water I mean, and it was just then I looked over and saw. She was wearing trousers, and there was blood on her socks, blood round the ankle, quite a lot, not like she'd hurt herself or anything either.'

He began to cry, his big face crumpling and his breath coming in heaves, a big, dry sort of crying, the worried harrumphing of a man who doesn't cry very often.

'I just lost it, Alison, I just thought, I don't want her in my car. And I pulled over. We'd just got past Burley Woods and I pulled into that stony bit by the Spinney at the top end and I said, get out. I've taken you far enough. You'll have to get someone else, get out.'

'What did she do?'

He stopped harrumphing. 'She went. She looked at me, then she turned and opened the door and she just went. That was it. She ran off, just took off.'

'Which direction?' I asked calmly.

He shook his head. 'I didn't want to know. I just turned the car round and came back. When I heard, I thought, it's her, I know it's her. Then I thought maybe not, but it was, wasn't it?'

He gave me a pleading look. 'Will the police think it's me? Will they think I done it? What if there's blood in the car? That's how people get put away for things they never did, you know, I've seen it on the box.'

I breathed out loudly, looking at the fields, then I turned and patted his forearm. 'It's okay,' I said vaguely. 'You were right not to tell anyone. It's okay.'

'Can you sort it out for me? Can you? I couldn't think who else. I don't know any solicitors. How do you get a solicitor?' His large face was pink with anxiety and his mouth had formed a childish moue.

I should have told him not to worry. I should have said that he wouldn't be in any trouble, that I would help him sort it out.

Instead, I said, 'You definitely haven't told anyone else?'

6

And Isaac spake unto Abraham his father, and said . . . Behold the
fire and the wood: but where *is* the lamb for a burnt offering?

Genesis 22: 7

*A*t what point did she know that the baby was evil?
She knew when it was still in the womb. From the
moment the doctor had announced her pregnancy, Joyce
Akenside had felt a coldness inside, a solid lump of knowledge
in her stomach that told her this was wrong.

'But I've got two already,' she heard herself saying to Dr
Carter, as if he didn't know. 'A boy and a girl,' she continued
lamely. She already had a boy and a girl. That was enough,
more than enough. She had one of each. What did she need
another one for?

Dr Carter was a genial man, never short-tempered like
some other doctors. There were decorative handles on his
filing cabinets. China cups and saucers teetered on the edge
of his battered wooden desk – a touch of unprofessionalism
which endeared him to his women patients. He drank tea.
He was a man with human needs.

'Well,' he said, 'two isn't really that many, you know,
although I know it's common to have only two these days.
You'll probably be surprised how easy it is now you've got
the hang of it. I wouldn't worry.' Silenced by his clumsy
reassurances, her tongue burned with the unuttered.

On her journey home, she stopped at The Teapot and
ordered a coffee. Normally, she did some shopping before
going to collect her youngest from nursery, but normality had

91

come crashing down. She needed to break her routine in order to prove to herself that this was really happening. She chose a window seat and sipped automatically, not realising she had drained the cup until she tipped nothing but air between her open lips.

Outside, the High Street was almost empty. The occasional young mother hurried by, raincoat-clad. Opposite The Teapot was Christopher's Hosiery and Fancy Goods and it occurred to her that the corners of her husband's handkerchiefs were tatty. The window of the shop announced that many items were reduced. She felt a fleeting rush of annoyance that it didn't say which. She would go in to buy handkerchiefs and come out with tea towels, which would be no good to Gordon at all.

People don't wear headscarves any more, she thought aimlessly. By 'people' she meant other mothers like herself. The vagaries of fashion did not often penetrate Oakham but she felt the whole pressure of the changing world in this one small detail. Now we must all walk around with unprotected heads, her thoughts continued, so that anything can get at us. She fingered the small gold cross she wore on a fine chain round her neck. It had been a Confirmation present from her father.

Dear Lord, she thought distinctly, and it was all she could do to prevent herself from bowing her head right there in The Teapot. I have asked for very little. I have done what I was supposed to do. I have given Gordon first a son, then a daughter. I have learnt how to make pastry. My one selfishness is the long baths I take and pretending to Gordon that Dr Carter told me they were necessary for my bad back. Perhaps you have done this to me because you thought I was becoming smug. I am twenty-six and things have turned out more or less how I expected. If so, I apologise and I can honestly say that I have learnt my lesson. But please, God, do not make me go through with this. You can stop it if you want. There are ways and means which will not be my fault. I will give you until the end of next week.

She opened her eyes. It was only then that she realised they had been closed. The world outside the window had not changed. The women still strode down the pavements, legs scissoring purposefully. Christopher's Hosiery and Fancy Goods was still holding its sale.

She rose from her seat, unclipping her purse and fingering the cold coins inside. The price of a cup of coffee had gone up to thirty new pence. It seemed appropriate that it was costly.

All babies were the same but different. This was what Joyce found so disturbing. Certain gestures were archetypal; the balled-up fist, the arching back – every baby in the history of babies had done those things. Each time one of her own children did, she was filled with irrational affection. But you're just a baby, she would think, gazing at her infant in surprise. That's all you are, after all.

The individual traits were more difficult to come to terms with, for then she was reminded that another person had entered her home, uninvited, through the portal of her unwilling body.

Her first-born was solid and sullen – everything a boy baby should be. When Andrew cried, his face reddened and his nose seemed to flatten, his mouth became twisted and ugly. He seemed as angry with himself as with the world around him. He fed furiously and screamed with colic every evening. You couldn't do a thing with him. He might have slid into the world at eight pounds exactly but having him around was like having a little hippo in the house, a noisy little hippo.

The girl was different; a slim baby, although not particularly pretty. From the start she hated to be cradled and was much happier upright against her mother's chest. As soon as she could hold her head up she would peer over Joyce's shoulder and look around, big-eyed, turning her head from side to side, like a prairie dog. Her favourite toy was a teething rattle made of ivory which Joyce had been given by Gordon's mother. It had a little metal bell on the end, which Alison chewed endlessly, so much so that she cut her lip a couple of times, although it never seemed to dim her affection for the thing. Joyce could leave her with it for ages in the pram on the patio. When she went to the sliding door to listen, she would hear the tinny tinkle of the bell floating on the wind.

Andrew screamed the whole morning long, a noise so loud and physical Joyce was surprised it didn't flip the cat net off the pram.

There was less than two years between them. Joyce was a firm believer in getting the toddler business out of the way as quickly as possible. If she had her children close together, they would at least be able to entertain each other at some point. Gordon had acquiesced. The babies had pleased Gordon's mother no end – she was a widow desperate to leave her small amount of savings to a worthy cause. Joyce loathed Gordon's mother but managed to conceal it until she was dead and buried, when she duly stood at the old bat's graveside and prayed that God would forgive her for accepting whatever few measly items she might have been left in her will.

Sure enough, the small amount of money went to the children. It was to sit in the Mowbray Building Society until they were both grown up, by which time it might possibly be worth something.

Joyce was left a black sewing-machine with mother-of-pearl-trimmed handles which folded down into its own bureau. She stored it in the garage.

The children seemed to like each other. Joyce praised the Lord. Andrew was strangely protective of his sister, leading her around as soon as she could crawl, as if she were a puppy.

When he started school, he would rush across the playground when they went to meet him and say, 'Alison, we did numbers today. We did the numbers. I'll show you.' He seemed entirely indifferent towards his mother, which suited her fine. Joyce had never really had any interest in boys.

When Alison started nursery, she would come home solemnly and say, 'New dress,' if anything had been spilt on the one she was wearing. The first time she saw a cake with chocolate vermicelli on it she said, 'Cake is dirty.'

With Andrew at school and Alison due to go there in the autumn, Joyce had begun to feel that at last her life was taking shape. She had produced a son and a daughter, and both were manageable. Her husband went to the pub a lot but usually slept in the box room when he came home drunk and didn't bother her.

With the family sorted out, she could now put her house in order. The pantry needed going through – there were tins of Golden Syrup that had been in there since she was pregnant with Andrew. The box room could be turned into her household room – maybe Gordon's mother's sewing-machine could be rescued from the cobwebs in the garage. She could make some new curtains for the lounge.

It was 1974 and everything else was going to the dogs. First there was the three-day week, thanks to the miners, then fights breaking out in petrol queues. So much was going wrong in the world. Joyce knew that God was punishing everybody, because of all that free love and women's lib. He had let that plane crash in Paris and hundreds of people had died, even if a lot of them were Turkish. Then there was that bomb on the bus, the soldiers and their children. The royal family was not exempt. But for the bravery of her husband and bodyguard, where would Princess Anne have ended up? Making omelettes for a lunatic in an underground bunker.

Even in Rutland, they were up in arms. Joyce couldn't understand the fuss. Cumberland and Westmorland had gone as well – the whole world was changing. It was God's way of trying to get people to see how sinful they had become. On the very day that Rutland disappeared, Joyce noted in the *Mirror*, family planning was becoming available on the NHS. Everybody's taxes were going to pay for the fornicatory habits of a few.

She herself had an ordered life. She couldn't help thinking how well she had made things turn out.

Pride was a sin. Later that month she discovered what her punishment was to be. It was Dr Carter who suggested the pregnancy test. She had only gone about her back. She hadn't had the curse for three months but that was not uncommon. Ever since Alison, things down there had been all over the place.

She had only let Gordon near her once that year, after three Martinis and lemonade in the Earl of Cambridgeshire. She didn't normally drink but it had been Ida's leaving do. Joyce and Ida had been neighbours for years. Ida was going to Australia. Now she was gone and Joyce's well-ordered life was in tatters. Another baby. It was a disaster.

When the new baby was due, Joyce went to All Saints, mid-week, as she liked to do. She attended the sung Eucharist with the children every Sunday but she also liked to go when the church was empty, on Wednesday afternoons usually. She liked to have God to herself for an hour or so.

Her pregnancy had hardly shown for most of it. Then, all at once, she had ballooned. Her first two had been high. She had had terrible heartburn. This one seemed small and low, squatting on her bladder, compressing it like a deflated bicycle tire. She had put on more weight than usual. As she walked down Church Passage, she could feel her thighs grazing together with a synthetic slither. The squeezing of her internal organs was a hot sensation. Her breath was short.

She paused by the noticeboard in the church porch. There

was a meeting, that Saturday, to discuss the latest edict from the Liturgical Commission. The vicar would be in attendance. Joyce didn't care for him much. He was too friendly. He signed his letter in the parish magazine, 'Your friend, Canon Jonathan'. Joyce had much preferred the old vicar, Reverend Savage, who was suitably obstreperous and ended up in a wheelchair with a tartan rug over his knees, as all vicars should.

Joyce thought that it would be nice to go along to the meeting and give her friend Canon Jonathan a piece of her mind but the baby would probably be out by then. The last two had been on time.

The noticeboard also had a programme of musical events for January and February, something to fill the post-Christmas void now that carol concerts were no longer appropriate. It wasn't just organ recitals these days. The County Minstrels were doing a selection from Gilbert and Sullivan. Whatever next?

She lifted the iron latch and swung the oak door open, stepping carefully over the wooden lip. As she clunked it shut behind her, the noises from the street disappeared and she was left with the brown echoey air and the layered scent of incense. God's talcum powder, her mother used to call it.

The church was empty, as usual. The air held a bitter chill, but even though she could no longer button her coat she didn't feel the cold. She rocked slowly down the aisle, dragging her feet on the flagstones. Her feet and ankles were so huge that she could no longer fit her heel into her shoes. Instead, she had broken the backs of them and had to shuffle everywhere, like a madwoman.

She eased herself into the second pew, her veined hand clutching the *fleur-de-lys*-shaped post for balance. She always sat in the second pew. It seemed impertinent to sit in the front, as if she were gentry. 'Know your place,' her father had told her, several times a day, throughout her childhood. It was the secret to happiness, knowing your place.

In front of her was the brass lectern, a huge thing in the shape of an eagle, wings spread to form a resting place for the Word of God. Its head was turned to one side and its beak agape. It had a single eye fixed upon her. Beyond the eagle was the altar, the small crucifix on the white cloth, and rearing above it the huge stained-glass windows – the shapes of Jesus and the disciples in brilliant blue and red.

Was any red so livid as the red shine of that glass? God was big and colourful, that was what kept her coming. Somewhere in her life, amidst the greys and browns of motherhood, there was a corner that was bright and hard.

She could no longer kneel comfortably. It was all right once you were down. It was the getting there and back up again that was the tricky bit. Anyway, she didn't feel all that humble. She rested both hands on the pew in front of her, her face raised.

Dear Lord, she said to herself, silently, although she hissed her thoughts with such resonance it seemed the same as speaking them out loud. I do not think You have been fair. I have been racking my brains and have finally come up with it. I was wrong to be so pleased with myself about how I had organised my life but You have got the punishment out of all proportion. I understand how this could be very easy to do, after all, there is a lot of wickedness to punish and it must be easy to get carried away. Killing the first-born son in every family, for instance. I think we can all agree that was a little unnecessary.

Joyce's God was very much an Old Testament God. She even preferred his old name, Yahweh. The word God meant so little these days – or so much. It had shattered into a thousand different Gods, each one peculiar and individual. Yahweh, on the other hand, was not open to interpretation. Yahweh knew his own mind. He had long pointy fingers and a stern brow. (He was the one that was a jealous God.)

Maybe it is just that there is something going on here that You have not yet seen fit to reveal, Joyce continued. I know that You could not be doing something like this to me without a good reason but You have left me to carry on all these months without giving me a clue as to what it might be. You brought Your only son into the world so that He might be sacrificed on a cross and we could all enter Your kingdom but that is likely to be some way off for me and anyway, I'm hardly Mary and Gordon's hardly Joseph, is he, forgive the levity. I know I should be praying for the soul of Nixon and everyone in his wicked, wicked country. I know that Mrs Moore round the corner whose husband stepped in front of the train on Boxing Day probably thinks I pray for her but at this particular point in time you might understand that I am thinking about myself. After all, in this condition, all you can do is wait. It's hard to do anything at all, except wait. So this is just to tell you, I'm waiting.

She paused, sitting up straight. There was a movement from inside her abdomen, a turning. The baby had not been doing much recently – things had clearly got a bit tight in there. She shifted her torso a little, to one side, then the other. There was also something else, a dull presentiment of pain in her lower back, a sensation both mild and ominous.

It was then that the voice came, cold as water, clear as stained light. She located its source before it finished speaking, even though it only spoke two sentences.

Wait, Mrs Akenside, and I shall show you what to do. You are the scourge of all evil.

She sat back in the pew, eyes wide, face pink with gratification. Yahweh had heard her, after all.

The eagle had spoken.

*   *   *

The new baby was different from the others. It was milky-eyed, opaque. Joyce knew there was a personality lurking in there somewhere – every mother knew that – but this baby seemed intent upon concealing it. It slept a lot, as though it couldn't be bothered to complain.

She had breastfed Alison and Andrew until they started teething. Andrew had drained her six times a day, putting on weight with such speed that his body grew in alarming disproportion to his tiny baby features. By six weeks, he had looked as though she had blown him up with a bicycle pump. In contrast, Alison's suckling had been demure. While she fed, her small grey eyes would gaze around the room. Once in a while, she would break off and look up at Joyce quickly, checking she was still there, as if someone else might have sneaked into her mother's place – Harold Wilson, say.

The new baby made no fuss about feeding. It simply wouldn't do it. It did not scream or kick the way babies who refused the breast usually did. It simply kept its lips clamped shut and turned its head away. They put it onto bottles and took away the water jug by the side of Joyce's bed so she would stop producing milk. She lay there with a raging thirst and breasts like party balloons for five whole days, until they let her home. Still, it saved a lot of fiddling with nursing bras.

Incubus and succubus. It was a trick. The baby thought if it refused to suck, maybe Joyce wouldn't notice. Perhaps it thought that clutching a bottle and puffing its little cheeks like bellows was endearing. Joyce wasn't fooled. She held it as it pulled at the bottle's latex teat and gazed down at the tiny, furry head, where a small rug of cradle cap nestled amidst the fine brown hairs. I am cleverer than you, she thought, because whatever you are, you are still a baby.

All babies were psychic. It was always possible to communicate your displeasure at them, providing you had the necessary skill and vehemence. Andrew, for instance, had been a terrible sleeper. He rummaged around in his cot all night long, even when he was swaddled, wriggling from one end to another like a desperate, human-headed slug. She would go in and grip the side of his cot and glare at him in the half-light. She always lit a nightlight and put it on the window-sill, then left the curtains open. That way, when the nightlight burned out in the middle of the night, there was still some light from the streetlamp. The alternative was to leave his door open and the landing light on but then she and Gordon were kept awake all night by his crying. She put up with it when he needed night feeds, but when he was big enough to go through until morning she thought it best to ignore him.

With the door open, the single bulb from the landing would shine dimly from behind her, throwing her bulging shadow over his tiny squirming form. Let . . . me . . . sleep, she thought, the words thundering in her head in fierce monosyllables, the consonants so clipped she was convinced that he could hear them even though she never spoke a word.

Faced with her anger, the pitch of Andrew's crying would at first increase, but if she slammed the door behind her after she left, it gradually subsided to a moan. Ten minutes later, he was asleep. Ever since then, she had realised that you didn't have to hit a child, just make them afraid.

A bitter January ended, folding into a February that was dark and mushy grey. Alison and Andrew were back at school and Joyce was alone with it, still waiting. She had stopped going to church. Mrs Moore round the corner had noticed and knocked on the front door one afternoon, invited herself in and said she had just come to check that Joyce didn't have the baby blues. Joyce had given her short shrift. She had no intention of going back to church until God got His act together and gave her some clue about what was going to happen. She told Mrs Moore she had a trapped nerve and the sour old dear pursed her lips with sympathy as Joyce levered her out of the door.

February died. March marched past. Still there was no sign.

Then, the evening came when she was on her own in the house with the children. Gordon had started on a spell of nights at the pea-podding factory just over the border, towards Grantham. It meant he was around getting under her feet during the daytime, but they needed the money.

At least she had the evenings to herself. She would let Alison and Andrew play in their rooms as long as they didn't disturb her – they put themselves to bed quite often these days. She bathed them in the mornings.

She was downstairs, in the lounge, feet up on the leather pouf which had been their only sales purchase that year. They hadn't had one before and she had been getting an inordinate amount of pleasure from it on the few occasions she had sat down.

She was on page four of the newspaper when it began, the unconvincing complaint of the baby. He had started doing it in the evenings, just in the last week or so. She had put him to bed less than an hour before.

She went upstairs, letting her feet thud lazily on the stairs, just to warn everybody she was coming. The door to the baby's room – the room that would have been her room – was on the right of the landing.

She stood over the cot.

It wasn't even crying properly. Its eyes and mouth were open but the sound that came out was ghostly, unreal, a pointy mewling like the Siamese kitten that Gordon's mother had bought, then promptly given to a neighbour because she couldn't stand the noise.

What was wrong with it this time? It couldn't be hungry – it had taken a whole eight ounces just before bed. It wasn't wind – it had croaked like a bullfrog all the way up the stairs. It wasn't the nappy either – after the feed Joyce had pinned a new terry tightly around its pale stomach, tucking the waistband of the plastic knickers over to prevent seepage. There was absolutely nothing wrong.

She gazed down at the baby. Its face was twisted with distress. Its eyes were half-closed and its arms flailing as it made clumsy, hapless efforts to put itself back to sleep. It turned its head from side to side, tormentedly. She watched.

Suddenly, it came to her, with all the clarity and brightness of the red light through the church's stained-glass window. That was it, of course. There was nothing wrong. That was why it was crying. She bent low and peered at it, moving the nightlight nearer the end of the window-sill so that she could look more closely at its inauthentically screwed-up face. It was a lonely little face, the face of someone who has realised that they are quite singular, and that they always will be. It was the face of a creature distressed by its own perfection.

And all at once, Joyce Akenside was overwhelmed with love for her baby, her second little boy, her James. She had believed him to be evil – and now she saw that the opposite was true. He was too good. She had thought that everything was wrong with him – and now she was certain he was too right. His tiny form would always be as unprotected as a snowflake. Snow-baby, she thought, gazing at him in the nightlight's cold, undimming glimmer. My perfect child.

She thought of all the things that would befall him, listing them in her head. How many wasp stings could a person expect to receive in one lifetime? How many grazed knees? How many sicknesses? Why was it not possible to bundle all these mishaps up into one and get them over and done with all at once? She knew that everybody had to suffer, because of original sin, but surely all the agony and unhappiness could be squeezed into one intense but finite period, when you were too young to remember it – then, perhaps, a life could be happily lived. Why could a mother not do that for her child, especially a child such as this?

This baby was too perfect. She knew that now. She stared down at it.

The Holy Spirit had spoken through the eagle in the church. Now she prayed that the Lord might show her what to do.

Suddenly, the baby stopped crying, and opened its eyes wide, wider than it had ever opened them before. It stared up at Joyce, and she saw Yahweh in that stare. The white, ovoid flame of the nightlight was twinned in its pupils. She drew in breath.

Could she succeed where Abraham had failed? Abraham had been let off the hook because he was a man. Typical. God couldn't have relied on Gordon to perform a ritual sacrifice on a burning pyre on a mountain in the land of Moriah. You couldn't trust Gordon to put the cat out.

Joyce straightened above the cot and closed her eyes, briefly. If, when she opened them, the baby had gone to sleep, she would leave the room.

When she opened her eyes, the baby was still looking at her.

She reached out a slow, purposeful hand. Its shadow passed over the cot, like a distant raven, but the baby did not blink. Silently, Joyce picked up the nightlight and moved it to the edge of the window-sill, within an inch of the open curtain. As she moved it, the flame bent and wavered, the tip clinging to its original position, as if it was unwilling to be displaced. She took a step backward. Who knew what would happen now? It was in the hands of God.

Already, the heavy weave of the curtain was beginning to crumple and darken.

She turned, thinking, Andrew and Alison are in their rooms. I must make sure they are both downstairs.

Andrew was not in his room, nor was he downstairs. He was standing in the open doorway of the baby's room. He was watching her. The landing light shone from behind and above him, so although she could tell his face was gazing up at her, she could not decipher its expression; except that the eyes were dark.

She strode roughly towards him, grabbed his shoulder and turned him round, pushing him out of the room. Then, without looking back, she closed the door behind her.

7

I made a detour on my way back from Market Overton, going via Cottesmore and Exton, then down Barnsdale Avenue, the old Viking Way. It feels like an invader's road, that road. It is straight, purposeful, and lined with huge trees that seem to grow towards each other and form a tunnel, a slipway to another time.

Pre-Christian hordes trampled all over this county. In the churchyard at Braunston there is the stone carving of a pagan fertility goddess. Nobody noticed for centuries that she was there. All that time, God-fearing folk had been strolling past her as they went in to worship.

I joined the A606 as it took a rash dive towards Oakham. Rutland Water twinkled flatly on my left. On the right, the green of Burley Wood bulged over the landscape.

Just past the brow of the hill, there is a lay-by, a patch of stony ground in front of a five-barred gate. The woodlands are private and there is a big sign with red lettering saying NO PUBLIC ADMITTANCE. Burley Wood is officially designated Ancient Woodland. As I parked the car, I thought about all the stories of woods which I remembered from my childhood; *Snow White*, *Beauty and the Beast*, the tales of Narnia with deer that talked and deer that didn't talk. (It was okay to eat the latter but not the former, I recalled.) There was one book, I remembered, about a young princess who was lost at night. The goblins in the wood were out to get her, lurking in the undergrowth by the side of the path. To stay safe from them, she had to walk very calmly and not be afraid. Not being afraid was important. If she broke into a run, they would get her.

I parked in the lay-by and got out of the car, leaving the door open. I was only going to take a quick look and I wanted to stay within sight of it. I told myself that I couldn't be bothered to lock the car and needed to keep an eye on it but I think it was more that I wanted it to be able to keep an eye on me. It was a modern object. It had acquired reassuring qualities.

On the opposite side of the road, the fields swooped down to the white and grey expanse of Rutland Water, glimmering so convincingly it was hard to believe it was a man-made reservoir. None of the water in it ends up in Rutland homes – it all gets piped to East Anglia. There was a big fuss when it was built, back in the seventies. Some prime farming land disappeared under all that water, along with a hamlet of several cottages. It was demolished, but I still think of it as being under there somewhere, a tiny English version of the Lost City of Atlantis. I remember Mum telling me about a Lions trip she went on, to look around the excavations, and how she thought, where will they get all the water from? How will they stop it draining away? Maybe she thought they would put a huge plastic tarpaulin underneath – weighted down with boulders, perhaps.

Now, there is a nature reserve; walks, sailing. The weekends are busy. Sometimes, you see the occasional Pakistani family, over from Leicester, being stared at by us locals as if they were a particularly interesting species of fauna. You can still live your whole life in Rutland without meeting anyone who has, as Miss Crabbe would put it, 'a bit of colour in them'.

Traffic passed intermittently, the cars roaring and fading. I was parked in an exposed spot and drivers coming up the hill from Oakham had a full view of me for a couple of miles. I would have to be quick.

I walked over to the gate and leant on the top bar, staring into the wood. The light was fading. There was the odd, pointless cheeping of a solitary bird.

The lay-by was at the top end of the woods. To one side there was the well-preserved glory of Burley Wood itself, divided by a barbed-wire fence from the small, scrubby afterthought of Ashpit Spinney.

I didn't know whether the Spinney counted as Ancient Woodland or not but it didn't look like it. Leading into the trees was a narrow, twin-furrowed track. Maybe the owner took a Land-Rover up there occasionally, to go shooting, perhaps, although I couldn't imagine there was much in there to shoot at. It seemed lifeless, dry and crackling. The trees were top-heavy and unkempt, the ground level overgrown with beige strands of tall dead grass. The track turned after a few yards and became lost. To the right, by the barbed-wire fence, there was a pile of old doors.

The dusk was quickening, the sky clouding over. The last remaining glow of sunlight was struggling through a gathering mass of lilac and grey. It was going to be another still night.

It was ten days since the Cowpers' murder and Gemma's flight from Nether Bowston courtesy of Tim Gordon's beaten-up motor. The stony lay-by was where she would have climbed out of the car. If she had walked along the A606 or tried to cross the open fields by Rutland Water, surely somebody would have seen her and reported her. She must have headed into the woods.

Burley Wood was swathed in barbed wire and obviously well managed, open. The Spinney was the only hiding place.

It takes weeks to starve but only days to die of dehydration – even I knew that. What was she drinking, rainwater? There had been no rain. There were probably stagnant ponds in the Spinney. Country legend has it that if you drink from a stagnant pond you go mad, but Gemma Cowper was mad already. Maybe it would send her sane.

What do you do if you are deranged and frightened and alone?

You pretend to yourself that you are hiding, when actually you are waiting to be found.

I gripped the splintered top bar of the gate, pursing my mouth, narrowing my eyes. I was not a brave princess. I had no intention of stumbling through trees in the darkness looking for a teenage psychotic in bloodstained clothing. At the same time, I knew that I couldn't let this knowledge go. I had something that nobody else had. There had to be some way to use it.

I glared into the Spinney, before turning and striding defiantly back to my car.

Now, sometimes, I look back to the way I stood at that gate as the light faded and try to remember what I was really thinking. What followed muddied everything. Did I really believe she was in there?

Maybe I only remember it that way because of what I know now. Sometimes I think, my thoughts cannot have been that logical or clear, whatever story I have made up for myself.

I don't think I really believed that she could still be in there after all that time.

WHERE IS GEMMA? The headline greeted me as I arrived at the office the next morning. It was Friday. Six copies of the *Record* were fanned neatly on the coffee table by the front door. We had hit the streets.

I had slept badly and rose early, creeping around the house so as not to wake Andrew who was comatose in my airless little box room. He had left his tin of tobacco and Rizlas downstairs, so I pinched them and sat on my back step, taking up smoking again while I had the opportunity.

It was early enough for the air to be damp, for the grass to glimmer. I loved that mistiness, the mingling of grey and green. The morning felt fresh in my lungs. When I inhaled, I could taste each mouthful of smoke.

I have a row of evergreens at the top of the slope that leads up to the end of the garden. Sitting on the step, I couldn't see the distant fields but I knew of them, knew they were there. There was space above me and beyond.

There was nothing in the garden when I moved in, just a few foxgloves hiding among the dandelions and cow parsley and a couple of sad dog roses which wouldn't flower for three years. I was hopeless to start off with, buying anything I liked the look of from the garden centre. I put in a whole row of delphiniums, which got eaten by snails. I didn't do a pH test on the soil. I didn't even use compost. On my first trip to the centre I took a list of the essentials, according to the beginner's book I had bought at the newsagent's. It said, 'And of course, you must have a pair of good stout gardening-shoes.' I thought that gardening shoes were something specific, like the shoes you need to go bowling, or ice skates. I wandered up and down the aisle of the garden centre's indoor bit, looking for them.

The stone step was cold beneath me. I had pulled on a skirt and t-shirt in a rush of optimism about how warm it was going to be that day. My skin prickled pleasantly. My arms were goose-pimply. I rubbed them. It reminded me of how they feel when I weed around my rose bushes. You can't help getting tiny, invisible cuts on your arms – the thorns are unavoidable. You don't notice it when you're hard at work. Then you go inside to get a drink of water and the sweat stings on your skin with a pain so minute it is exquisite. You know you are alive.

I breathed the damp air and finished my roll-up. I hugged

myself and listened to the skittering of a bird, twisting unseen in the back border.

I watched my lawn. It needed scarifying. I wondered what to do.

My life before the murders seemed long ago and far away. I suppose it is the same with any dramatic event. Time contracts, then explodes. I thought, I haven't seen anyone for ages – friends that is; Lizzie, my badminton buddy; Pat from school. The three of us go to the pub occasionally. Pat had a fling with Andrew once and I had been wondering whether we should all go out for a drink while he was around.

Now, though, I could only concentrate on one thing. It burned in my head. I had something, some knowledge that no one else had – not even Tim Gordon, whose imagination went no further than his timidity would allow.

WHERE IS GEMMA? Supposing I was right? It was a story. I had inside knowledge. Knowledge is power. A little knowledge is a dangerous thing. Villain, know thyself. How often in my lifetime would this kind of thing happen to me?

I drove to work listening to the radio. Most of it was election garbage but there was also a report on the breakdown of the nuclear family. Stabbing your parents to death – that's a pretty unequivocal way to break up your family. I realised I hadn't seen much cultural analysis of the case yet, not even in the broadsheets. Maybe somebody would be interested in a big feature. How much would a national newspaper pay for something like that? I had no idea. Enough to get my re-wiring done? A tabloid would pay, surely. I earned £9,560 per annum. I had a mortgage I could scarcely afford and months of remedial works to pay for. I had no real interest in working for a national newspaper – I much preferred being a big fish in little Oakham – but it did occur to me that I could try and develop a profitable sideline, something that brought in a bit of extra money without any commitment.

I thought about it for the rest of that morning. I thought

about it as I sat at my desk reading through some of Cheryl's interview notes. She had done a lot of the background on the Cowper case that week. She was good at that. She had tracked down the local doctor who had signed their death certificate, talked to Gemma's old schoolteachers. You would not call Cheryl one of the great prose stylists but you could always rely on her to come up with the facts.

Doug was standing in front of my desk.

'Do you think we should do something on the progress of the search?' I asked him. 'You know, maybe a map of where she could be, ask John about each area. Something to get people going. We could use some of that stuff John told you, maybe.'

Inspector Collins had confided in Doug after the press conference, off the record of course. There was bad blood between him and the fat super – not surprising, really.

Doug downturned the corners of his mouth, looking pettish. 'We'd have to dress it up. We don't want to drop John in it.'

'What about this bloke in the car?' I asked, without looking up from my papers.

'He thinks it's a dud. He thinks she's in one of the barns. They're doing Wardley Wood and Quakers Spinney over the weekend.'

I picked up a biro and twiddled it. 'They'd better get a move on, hadn't they? What about Burley Wood?'

Doug lifted his arms, bent at the elbow, and eased his shoulders backwards, as if he had a twinge of indigestion. 'He's having problems. Like I said, this super's trying to do it on the cheap and of course John knows but this bloke won't listen. They've got the RAF in to do Rutland Water 'cause it looks good on the telly. He's tearing his hair. They'll have to do Burley soon, they'll look daft otherwise. The super's got the personnel on house-to-house in the villages.

113

John's furious. He said it's not as if she'd've checked into a B and B, is it?'

Doug got to his feet and picked up a wooden ruler from my desk. 'They say that the old man bought it in the stomach, like this.' He gestured with the ruler, a straight stabbing motion level with his waist. There was something comic about Doug's plump white forearm making such a movement, clutching the wooden ruler like a schoolboy. 'Which I suppose is conceivable from the girl. She was five foot six and her dad was only two inches taller. The mum was about the same height and she was stabbed like this.' He raised the ruler up above his head to jab downwards, then froze in that position.

I thought, for a moment, that he was striking a pose. I only realised what was happening when I looked at his face and saw it was rigid with pain, the eyes tight closed, the mouth cracked open.

I was on my feet in one speedy, fluid movement – a movement which seemed all the more efficient in comparison with his clumsy collapse. He was pitching forward, arm still raised. I rounded my desk but wasn't in time to catch him. I reached out and grabbed at his shirt as he fell. His weight pulled it out of my hand and there was a harsh rasping as a seam gave.

After the ambulance had left, the mood in the office was strange. Cheryl went with Doug. They insisted on taking him over to Leicester, fully conscious and protesting furiously. I was in charge.

Everyone's concern for him was mingled with a guilty, holiday feel. It was Friday. The paper was out and the boss and his deputy were absent. I was up to my eyeballs in work but fidgety as a ferret. Cheryl had told me to ring Shires Periodicals and explain the situation. She and I could bring in next week's paper but if Doug was going to be off work for a while, they would have to send some help. Apparently, she and Doug had been requesting extra editorial and Shires Periodicals knew he wasn't healthy. I was surprised they hadn't discussed it with me. They must have known I wouldn't have minded a bit more editing.

All day, other members of staff came up to my desk and asked me to relate what had happened. All day we murmured and tutted. 'It never rains but it pours,' said one of the girls from production, meaning *first a murder, now this*. A mood of fatalism had descended and on its heels came a certain gaiety, an air of what-the-hell.

What-the-hell was how I felt when David Poe appeared. 'Hi,' he said. 'I heard about the ambulance. Is he okay?'

I shrugged, leaning back in my chair. 'We think so. They didn't have to resuscitate him or anything. I don't know.'

After a few minutes, I said, 'I can't really chat now. Do you want to go for a drink this evening?'

He looked pleased and surprised.

'What do you think I should do if I wanted to write a big piece about all this?' I asked him. 'What if I had a story?'

He looked at me. Between us on the pub table were two baskets with the glistening remainders of a meal. Shreds of grey flesh hung from the chicken bones. The chips were cold and limp. In each basket, there was a single lettuce leaf.

David Poe was on his third pint of County. I had had a Guinness, then moved on to vodka and lime. For some reason, he found it amusing that I drank vodka and lime. 'It's what all the girls at university used to drink,' he said, which offended me. It made me feel provincial.

Now, an air of intimacy had descended. I thought maybe he fancied me. I didn't fancy him, but there isn't a great deal of opportunity for flirting in Rutland, so I was making the most of it.

'So you're thinking of moving on to higher things?' he asked.

I frowned. 'You're making a typically metropolitan assumption.'

He spread his hands.

'You ought to realise, you lot,' I said, lifting my glass, 'you ought to have cottoned on by now, that everybody in this town knows exactly what you think of them. What you don't seem to appreciate is that the contempt is mutual.'

He rocked a little in his seat. 'Okay okay, point taken, so why don't you write this piece for the *Record*? I shouldn't think they'd be happy about you doing it for someone else, anyway.'

I shook my head. 'God, no. I'd get the sack. I'd have to use a pseudonym.'

'There's a lot of stuff been written already you know . . .' This was his tactful way of saying, why would a national newspaper buy a feature from a provincial hack like you?

I felt quite sober. 'What if I had a new angle?' I asked.

He didn't pick up on what I had said. He waved a hand. 'Everybody's got an angle. In London, the streets are paved with angles.'

The moment passed. The conversation moved on.

It wasn't until the end of the evening, when we were back out in the market place, that I raised the subject again.

We were standing by my car. Was I okay to drive? he wanted to know. We both knew I was way over the limit.

I fingered my car keys, ignoring his concern. 'So you don't think I should make a few phone calls, then?'

He sighed, clearly frustrated that the conversation had not remained on the intimate level he had spent all evening achieving. 'I don't think you'd get a commission unless they knew you, and it's pointless doing it on spec'.'

'What about information?' I asked. 'The tabloids pay for that, don't they? Let's say we forget the article.'

He paused and looked at me. I could almost hear the cogs in his brain turning.

'What sort of information?'

I shrugged. 'Something big enough for a front page.'

It was dark now. The air was cold, just to remind us that summer was not yet upon us. I thought how strange it was that the evenings seemed chilly, yet at night it was always so close. I shivered.

David Poe was biting his bottom lip. Two other journalists emerged from the pub behind us and we were silent while they passed us.

'I did a piece for the *Express* last year,' he said, measuredly. 'They were running a series of features on extra-marital affairs and someone I knew had a cleaner who had met her husband at a woodwork evening class. They were both married to other people at the time. She was supposed to be making a doll's house at this class but was having sex with this bloke in the back of his Fiesta. At the end of the course, they had to knock a doll's house up bloody quick. It was quite a nice little story. About eight hundred words, got subbed down to five. I got four hundred for writing it and permission from the editor to offer the cleaner up to a hundred and fifty so we could name her and get a good pic. I tried a hundred and she took it.'

I shook my head. 'That won't do it. This particular bit of information is worth a lot more than a hundred quid. I'd want to write a big, investigative piece. And I wouldn't want anyone subbing it, either.'

He pulled an amused face, then put on an American accent and said, 'Everyone gets subbed, honey. That's life in the big city.'

'But what if I had something really good?' I insisted.

He exhaled. 'Such as?'

'Police incompetence,' I said, 'and, maybe, Gemma's whereabouts.'

He opened his mouth in a silent, *ah* . . .

I felt a small flush of triumph. David Poe thought he had me all taped, some little rural eccentric. Now he was having to think again.

He lifted an arm and scratched the back of his head. 'I think maybe we should discuss this over a nightcap,' he said. 'I'm at the Stag.'

The Stag Hotel was just around the corner. A nightcap? Miss Crabbe's line occurred to me: I'm not as green as I'm cabbage-looking.

I shrugged, turned.

I've only stayed in a hotel for business once. It was a Posthouse somewhere near Coventry. Shires Periodicals was having a conference on Local News Gathering: Its Purpose and Implementation. Doug sent me, as 'the *Record*'s representative on earth'. He didn't regard it as a perk. Somebody had to go, and he and Cheryl both loathe all that corporate stuff. Doug calls all upper management 'trouser-pressers'. I had always assumed it was a sexual slur, until I stayed in the Posthouse Coventry.

I thought the conference was great fun – chatted up the Managing Editor, one George Bloomfield, had a room-service breakfast both mornings and power showers twice a day. I haven't got a shower at home.

The Stag Hotel was rather different from a Posthouse. David Poe's room was tiny and oddly shaped – a small square with a little corridor leading to a bathroom. The windows were leaded and the curtains heavily frilled. The bedspread had a huge floral pattern which reminded me of my old quilted dressing gown. Two plump pillows sat atop it, like Tweedledum and Tweedledee. On the opposite side of the room there was a dresser with a lace-covered tray; china cup upturned neatly on its saucer, a small white teapot, a glass dish with sachets of coffee and sugar and hot chocolate and little cartons of cream.

He opened the dresser doors to reveal – miraculously – a mini-bar. He opened it with a tiny key and knelt before it, his face made sickly by the glow from its interior.

'No brandy,' he said sadly. 'They've not been too hot on re-stocking. There's plenty of Smirnoff. Don't know what you'll mix it with. Orange juice? Tonic?'

'Tonic,' I said, seating myself on the end of the bed. The armchair next to the dresser was heaped with a briefcase, newspapers, clothes.

'No ice either I'm afraid,' he said as he poured my drink, gesturing towards a small plastic bucket with a fake wood-graining surround. 'There's never been any ice.'

As he handed me my drink and took a sip of his own, he grinned to himself. 'Here, take a look at this.' He bent down to the lower shelf of the wicker bedside table. 'Just to prove I'm not making it up.'

He handed me a copy of *Country Interiors* magazine. On the front cover was a picture of swathes of coloured fabric and the title of the lead article: *The A–Z of Gingham*.

'Classifieds, at the back,' he said.

I flicked through. He took the magazine from me and sat down beside me on the bed. 'Look,' he said, handing it back and pointing at an advertisement. He leant slightly closer than was necessary.

It was an advertisement for your own Gnome-making kit. Moulds for plaster of paris, enamel paints – and a small fishing rod. £16.99.

I smiled and said, 'Yeah, yeah, you might want one one day.'

'Do you blame people for taking the mickey?' he replied, smiling back.

I held on to the magazine, pretending to flick through it. It gave me something to do.

After a long pause, he took the magazine from my hands and put it down on the floor.

119

'So,' he said, lifting a hand and stroking my upper arm with the back of one finger, 'tell me your story.'

For a moment, I thought he meant my life story. I felt a brief flush of panic. He was that keen already? What on earth would he think when he met my mother?

Then I realised he was talking business. I wanted to move away from him, to discuss it more dispassionately, but to have moved at that point would have signalled rejection. I was not yet certain what I wanted to do.

'I think I know where Gemma is, might be.' I said. 'I'm not sure, of course, but I think so. It's going to make the police look pretty stupid. The investigation is all over the place.'

As he moved closer towards me, the ancient springs beneath us creaked and the bed undulated. The shifting of his weight made me tip and wobble. His breath washed against my right ear.

I was still holding my vodka and tonic. I took a large gulp and felt instantly sober. The natural thing would have been to turn towards him as I spoke, but our faces were too close together.

He took his finger away from my arm. The flesh stung lightly where he had been stroking it. He transferred his weight and rested the other hand, carefully, on my thigh. Each gesture was a progression, a slow advancement which gave me ample time between each step to signal acceptance or dislike. There was no middle ground. Indifference would be taken as affirmation.

His hand was warm, the way that soil feels warm when you pause from digging a border to kneel and break it up it in your hand. It feels warm even though you know it is cold.

I hadn't slept with anyone since I broke up with Martin, my last boyfriend, nearly three years ago. He was floor manager at the Farmwear Clothing warehouse on the Pillington Industrial Estate at Cold Overton.

'So, how did you work it out?' David Poe said, languidly.

The fingers of the hand which was resting on my thigh began to tighten and flex, as if he was preparing to knead it. He shifted his weight towards me so that the only comfortable thing I could do was lean back against the wall.

I rested back on my elbows, looked him full in the face and said. 'I haven't *worked it out,* as you put it.' I paused for effect. 'I've had a tip-off, from somebody who has seen her since the murders.'

The hand was suddenly still. His expression did not change. 'You can confirm this?' he asked. His voice was higher, quicker.

I sat up and he moved away. 'Yes, of course I can. What did you think I was talking about?'

He sat back and blew air through his lips. 'I thought . . . I don't know . . . a hunch or something. I didn't know you meant – you mean you *really* know where she is? Where?'

'Yes,' I insisted. 'And I'm not telling you, so just forget it. I'm not telling you anything. I just want to know whether you'll put me in touch with somebody who wants this story.'

He stood up and walked to the other side of the room. He leant against the wall and was silent for a moment, then he walked back and picked up his drink from where he had left it on the bedside table. He sat down on the bed again, then turned to face me.

'Alison, look, I'm as ambitious as the next bloke so I'm not saying I blame you, but this is an ongoing investigation. If you're serious, I mean really know, as opposed to taking a guess or hearing a rumour or something, no editor is going to touch this with a bargepole. It's an ongoing *murder* investigation. Perverting the course of justice. It's a criminal offence.'

'Bollocks,' I spat. 'If you knew, you'd use it fast enough.'

'No,' he said firmly, 'I wouldn't.'

We faced each other, sitting at either end of the plump,

creaky bed. I didn't know what to say next, so I said, 'I'm going to use your loo.'

The bathroom had no window. As I turned the light on, an extractor fan began a low, resonant humming which sounded both near and far away. I went to the loo and flushed the toilet, then ran a bowl of water to wash my hands.

On the sink, there was a tiny round soap, still in its paper wrapper. I pulled the wrapper off and turned the soap over and over between my damp hands. It smelt of apples and detergent.

The light above the mirror was a small fluorescent strip shaded by a curve of brass. My face looked yellow. My fringe was overgrown and I was constantly having to brush it back with my hand. The gesture made me look nervous.

The mirror was big enough for me to glance down my body – the white t-shirt over the pleated skirt. It was the first time I had worn a skirt without tights that spring. It wasn't really hot enough, but the warmth of the past couple of weeks had made me dig out my summer wardrobe. I was sick of winter clothes, the jumpers and leggings. When I had pulled on the skirt that morning, my legs had seemed so pale, the flesh chickeny. Now that it was cold and dark outside, I felt silly and wanted to be wearing something more comfortable.

I surveyed myself; the 100 per cent cotton, the flat shoes. I thought of the women David Poe must know in London, women who didn't let their fringes grow too long.

When I rejoined him, I saw that the atmosphere had changed. He had moved his clothes and papers off the armchair and put them down on the floor. He was sitting looking thoughtful, his elbows resting on the arms of the chair and the tips of his fingers pressed together so that his hands formed a pyramid in front of him. The posture annoyed me. All his posturing did.

'So,' I said, sinking down onto the bed, casually flirtatious, 'I suppose a fuck's out of the question now?' I was angry that I had lost the opportunity to turn him down.

He looked at me. 'Alison, who are you?' It was a simple question, said without malice, which made it all the more insulting.

I laughed nastily. 'Oh, sorry, you think all girls who live in small country towns should be sweet girlies with no opinions who are happy to unbutton their gingham smocks for hugely important journalists like you.'

'No,' he said quietly. 'That's not what I meant.'

'I think it is.'

We had reached an impasse. Somehow, I had to leave his room with dignity, preferably with a passing witticism. I rose and looked around for my jumper, which I had dropped somewhere as we came in.

He did not move from his chair. As I found the jumper and pulled it over my head he said, 'So what are you going to do?'

It occurred to me that if he was so high-minded he might report me to the police. If it was all an act and he was as much of a skunk as most national journalists, maybe he would tip off another paper, have me followed.

'I'll think about it over the weekend,' I said neutrally. 'Maybe I'll ring you on Monday.' I had no intention of calling him.

'It isn't me you should be ringing.'

I wanted to tell him he was a sanctimonious git; a hypocrite like my mother; a superior jerk like Doug and Cheryl, who always act like I'm the new kid on the block even though I've worked for them for years; a smug oaf like all the people in Oakham who spend their lives collecting opinions in the same way others collect beer mats. I hated him and all of them. I was sick to death of people who thought they knew me.

He rose and opened the door for me as I left. Absurdly, we wished each other pleasant dreams.

*   *   *

123

Andrew was still up when I got home. He was watching television with the lights off, slumped sideways on my settee, bathed in ghostly flickers. He had found a bottle of red wine in my pantry and was drinking it out of a plastic tumbler.

'You can have a proper glass, you know,' I said softly as I settled down onto the floor beside him. He handed me the tumbler without speaking. The sound on the television was low.

'You've just missed the best line in the whole film,' he said. 'You could have used it somewhere. It was great.'

I took a slug of wine. 'What is it?'

'Francis Ford Coppola, I think. *The Conversation*.'

'Who?'

'Gene Hackman is a bugging expert. He thinks he's responsible for some people being killed. He has nightmares. I've seen it before. It all turns on a misinterpretation. It's really clever.'

I leant forward and peered at Gene Hackman's brown leather jacket, the lapels, his flares. 'How old is this?'

'Seventies. But the line, it's great. I thought of you. He says, Gene Hackman, he's thinking about these people who have been killed and he says, "I'm not afraid of death, but I am afraid of murder."'

I nodded. 'Good line.'

'Where have you been, anyway?' He reached down and retrieved the tumbler.

'Nowhere. The pub. They had a lock-in.' I didn't want to tell Andrew about David Poe, or what I knew about Gemma. I knew he wouldn't approve. He's so moral.

'I should've rung you, I suppose. You could have come over on my bike.'

'Nah,' he said. 'I'm broke . . . Ugh.' He winced at a scene on the telly.

*   *   *

When the phone rang the following morning, I thought it was David Poe.

I was in the kitchen. I left my mug of tea and moved swiftly into the sitting room. Perhaps he was going to apologise.

It took me a moment or so to locate the phone. Andrew had been using it and left it lodged just underneath the settee. I extracted it carefully, as if I was coaxing a dog. It is an old Bakelite one. There is a slight hum on it. Through the hum, a voice I didn't recognise said, 'Alison?'

'Yes.'

'Alison, it's George Bloomfield here.'

I sat up, even though he couldn't see me. George Bloomfield was the Managing Editor of Shires Periodicals – my boss's boss. The conference in Coventry was the only time I had had a conversation with him that had lasted longer than two minutes. Apart from that, I had only met him a handful of times. He was fond of dropping in on our office unannounced to tell us what a wonderful job we were doing. He was so important he was on first name terms with everyone. He always talked in a way that suggested he was thinking, isn't it amazing I'm so gracious and polite?

He was *very sorry* to be ringing me at home on a Saturday. He hoped he wasn't spoiling my morning. After all, we had all done such a *wonderful* job with that week's newspaper we deserved a weekend off. He had been *so* sorry to hear about Doug. It must have been a terrible shock to all of us. Actually, he was ringing because he was going to be passing through Oakham on Tuesday morning and wondered if it would be possible to meet me somewhere for coffee. He would have suggested Monday but things were a little hectic over in Coventry and he was going to be in meetings all day. He wished he could make it lunch but he had to be in a meeting in Stamford at twelve noon. He would come by the office at eleven, but could I *possibly* think of somewhere nearby where he and I could go for a chat?

125

What's wrong with the coffee we serve in the office? I thought. There's plenty wrong with it, actually, but it had never seemed to bother him before.

We talked about the Cowper case, then he rang off.

I went through to the kitchen and got my mug, then came back to the phone. I didn't have Cheryl's home number but I knew she would be in the book.

She answered the phone immediately.

'Hi, it's Alison,' I said. 'How's Doug?'

'Oh he's going to be okay, you know. It was another little one apparently. He was lucky. Next time it'll be the biggie. I spoke to him just now. I'm going over later. He says they're talking about letting him out in a day or two. I can't believe it. I don't know whether they know there's no one to look after him.'

She sounded strained. She and Doug had known each other for so long. Anyone would look at him and know what would happen one day – the huge stomach, the florid features – he was a coronary waiting to happen.

I always think that fat people seem more alive than the rest of us. They take up more space, use more air. It seems bizarrely just that their lives should be shorter. I realised I had not taken Doug's heart attack that seriously because it seemed inconceivable that anything serious could happen to him. Surely the *Record* would fold up? Surely a hole would open up in the ground and the offices disappear into it?

I said, 'I've just had a call from George Bloomfield. He wants to have a coffee with me on Tuesday. What do you think he wants?'

There was a long pause.

When Cheryl spoke, her voice was cold and mild. 'Alison, I'm sure you can work it out.'

I realised I had rung her because I was excited and wanted to share it with her. She knew it. She was chastising me.

I didn't know what to say. It wasn't my fault Doug was ill.

'Well, say hi to Doug from me,' I said, eventually.

'Yes,' she said. 'Of course.'

I finished my tea, sitting on my sitting room floor with my back against the settee. Andrew had taken all the cushions upstairs to make up his bed. I wondered whether to take him a drink. I was almost out of herbal teas.

I only had a day or two, at most, before the police got their act together and searched Burley Wood. I had to do something. I stood.

A few minutes later I was at the kitchen window, rinsing my mug, when I saw the taxi draw up. The passenger was in the front seat, talking to the driver. I peered. I couldn't see who it was until she opened the door and began to clamber out, with all the large-limbed awkwardness of someone who is not accustomed to getting in and out of cars. I had just enough time to go to the bottom of the stairs and shout up to Andrew.

He came to the landing, rubbing his face with the heel of one hand. He was wearing an old towel and an expression of sleepy irritation.

'What?'

'It's *Mum*,' I hissed urgently. 'She's getting out of the taxi now.'

He gave me a look that encapsulated the whole of our childhood and adolescence in one appalled, wide-open stare. Then he disappeared back into the box room and closed the door behind him. There is no window in that room. I imagined him plunging himself into darkness, then climbing under the sheets and blankets and pulling them over his head. This is the man who hitchhiked solo the length of South America.

My mother was wearing the inevitable headscarf, even though it was a cloudless, sunny morning.

I hadn't visited my parents for some weeks and in the intervening period I had forgotten, as I always do, how physically unpleasant my mother is. She is a big woman with a taut, bony face which reminds me of those elderly trophy wives you see on television moguls' wives – women who have had so many facelifts you can almost see their skulls shining through their fleshless features. My mother has achieved that look without spending a penny. Perhaps it is so much prayer.

At the same time, it is clear from a single glance that she is a poor man's wife, a wife who has not been cherished. Her skirts cling to the fullness of her hips – her V-neck jumpers are saggy and bobbled. She is always clean, but never new.

She stood on the threshold of my cottage, not greeting me, untying the headscarf with calm but inefficient fingers. She pulled it smoothly from her head and her hair crackled to life.

It was only when she had folded the headscarf and pushed it under the flap of her handbag that she looked at me and said, 'Hello, Alison. Your father doesn't know I've come. I've come to see Andrew.'

I stepped back to allow her in, playing for time. Once inside my sitting room, she opened the handbag and withdrew a folded copy of the *Mirror*. She held it out to me.

'It's him, isn't it?' It was several days old. Andrew's photofit was on the front page. 'I didn't think it was him when they thought it was him that did it. He's still my boy. Then they did a report the next day saying he was someone visiting someone in the village. That's when I knew. Is he still here? Don't tell me he's gone when he hasn't. He's my son. I have a right.'

I wondered if she had noticed that the cushions were missing from the settee.

'He was around . . .' I said. 'Come through and I'll make you a cup of coffee.'

'I don't want coffee,' she snapped, and I looked at her in surprise. She is rarely that vehement.

As I looked at her, the expression on her face changed. Suddenly, it softened, almost sagged. All at once, she went from middle-aged and furious to vulnerable, and old.

Andrew stood at the top of the stairs. He had pulled on a pair of combat trousers and a vest t-shirt. He was smoking ferociously. His other arm was wrapped round his body as if his t-shirt needed holding to his chest. His body language screamed, *leave me alone*.

'Hello, Mum,' he said, after a pause.

How long was it since they had seen each other? Twelve, thirteen years? How different would he look to her? Or would she only see the truculent teenager whose parting shot had been to tell her she was mad and stupid?

Her voice was low. 'I've come to talk to you, Andrew. I know you don't want to see me. You've made it quite clear. But there's things I want to talk about. You can leave afterwards. I won't bother you again.'

Andrew did not change position. 'What do you want to talk about?'

I felt like climbing the stairs and giving him a good hard slap. How could he be so unkind? Couldn't he make an effort, once in thirteen years?

My mother turned to me. 'Alison,' she said, 'I want to talk to Andrew on my own.'

Andrew stared down at me in alarm.

''Course you do, Mum,' I said pleasantly. 'Of course. I've got to go out, anyway. I can come back later if you like, give you a lift back.'

'It's all right,' she said. 'I've got a card. He gave me a card. Andrew can ring for me.'

I ran upstairs and got my bag and a jacket from my

129

bedroom, shouldering past Andrew, who was glued to the top banister, as saggy and immobile as the men we used to make out of Play-do when we were children. I didn't look at him. I had been dealing with Mum on my own for thirteen years. Now it was his turn.

As I descended the stairs again I said to him over my shoulder, 'I'll be back later. Before lunchtime probably.'

'Got to do some urgent shopping, have you?' Andrew muttered, furious that I was leaving him on his own.

I had reached the bottom of the stairs. I glanced up at him witheringly. 'It's work, actually.'

'Sorry,' said Andrew sarcastically. 'I forgot how important you are.'

I thought he was being unnecessarily unpleasant. It wasn't my fault Mum had turned up. I had protected him for over a decade. When was he going to grow up?

As I left, they were still standing in the same positions; Andrew hunched and sullen at the top of the stairs, Mum defiantly deranged at the bottom.

As I backed my car down the lane, I felt determined, in charge of my life. My family is pitiable, I thought. My mother had used a terrible accident during our childhood to ruin her whole life. I knew that I could not understand the scope or texture of her suffering. How could I imagine what it was to lose a baby? But she had done nothing to save herself. Instead, she sat in corners and raised us to be frightened of her. It was her own fault if neither of us liked her now. She was so helpless. It is impossible not to despise helpless people.

As I turned the car, I saw a crow sitting in the centre of the road. I paused, waiting for it to spread its wings, but instead it hopped disdainfully onto the grass verge, towards the shade, out of the sunshine that flooded the lane with unoriginal, bathetic light.

8

'Tell me about Lorrimer. What was he like?'

P. D. James
Death of an Expert Witness

Crows were vile. Crows weren't even ravens. Ravens were just as sinister but at least they were majestic. Ravens guarded the Tower of London, after all. They stopped it falling down.

In her youth, Edith Cowper (*née* Barnacle) had been described as having raven hair. She had worn it long then. It dropped about her face in a smooth, puffy swoop. Now only the face was smooth and puffy. The hair was short and crinkly. When she was young, it had been said of her, 'Edith will be beautiful when she is older.' Now she had turned fifty, she imagined others saying, 'I bet Edith was lovely when she was young.'

She held the poetry book in her hand and turned it over. *Crow*, it was called. On the front was a ghastly black shape. Why did the school give Gemma rubbish like that to read? Blood and guts and tiny, tiny poems with short hard lines – some lines were just one word. That wasn't a poem. Poems were long and fluid, falling like water. They shouldn't be a stab of syllables like all this modern rubbish.

She replaced the book carefully where she had found it, on Gemma's bedside table. Gemma was in the fifth year, sixteen years old. Edith couldn't think where they were going to get the money to see her through her A-levels. The school fees were crippling them, but Thomas was insistent. Nothing but the best for Gemma. Her exams were coming soon. Then, Thomas said, they would see that all that sacrifice had been worthwhile.

Edith sat down on her daughter's bed. It was such a pretty blue, that duvet. They had chosen it together from Rackham's in Leicester, years ago. Gemma had still been at primary school. They had talked to each other then, gone on shopping trips on Saturdays. They had had a relationship unfiltered by Thomas's ambitions for his daughter.

It was some time after Gemma had gone to secondary school that Edith began to realise that she had lost her. Gemma started to take herself so seriously, herself and her books. She became Thomas's child. She and Edith didn't go shopping together any more – they hardly spoke to one another.

Instead, Edith knew, her husband was teaching their daughter to despise her.

It started with the games.

During the week, they would watch the box. Gemma would be sent off to bed mid-evening, then Edith and Thomas would catch the news. Afterwards, Edith made a hot drink while Thomas knelt in front of the television changing channels.

At the weekends, there would be a break in the routine, partly because the news was never on at the right time. This seemed to liberate them. Sometimes, they would not put the television on at all.

The games were limited while Gemma was young. It was mostly cards; gin rummy, German whist – sometimes it was snap, although that made Gemma a little over-excited.

One evening, she taught them a new game, one she had learnt at school.

She was in the first year, and coming home each day bubbling with newness. Sometimes it was a fact. 'Snails are neither male or female, Mum. They're both.' Sometimes it was an observation. 'When the teacher puts us in threes it's quite good because you all have to work but if it's fours then there's always one who doesn't do anything.' Sometimes, she would simply glow with knowledge, as if everything she was absorbing was lighting her up from the inside. Edith was often at the kitchen window when Gemma came home from school. She would watch her walk down the drive. There was a freshness about her gait, a floatingness. Edith would gaze at her with awe, thinking, she is our ambassador – our oxygen supply.

The new game was called Cheat. Gemma had learnt it one lunchtime, she said, from two boarding pupils called Lynne and Tamsin. Normally the boarders didn't speak to the day girls. They were, Gemma said, stuck up.

Each player was dealt an equal number of cards. The object of the game was to get rid of them. The players took turns to put several of them in the middle of the table, face down, while announcing what they were; three twos, two jacks, four aces. If the person on your left called you a cheat, you had to turn the cards up. If you had been telling the truth, they had to take the cards, plus any other cards that were already on the table. If you had been lying, the cards were all yours.

Gemma won the first two games hands down. Early in the third game, when it seemed that all three of them still had fistfuls of cards, Thomas suddenly put four cards down on the table and declared, 'Four fives! I've won!' and lifted both hands to show that they were empty.

'Cheat!' Gemma and Edith chorused in unison.

Gemma reached out a hand and turned up the cards, spreading the four fives across the table with a disbelieving expression. 'But you had *loads* a minute ago . . .'

Thomas was sitting with his lips pressed together and his eyes lifted to the ceiling, his face fixed in an exaggerated, supercilious smile. His arms were crossed. He shrugged.

There was a moment's pause, then Gemma guessed. She

rose and went over to where her father was sitting and gave him a push with one hand. Thomas, still grinning, levered his weight so that he would not budge. She pushed again and managed to shift him slightly, to reveal the wad of cards he had slipped underneath his thigh while Gemma and Edith were examining their own.

Gemma grabbed them and threw them on the table. 'Dad,' she shouted, 'that's *cheating*!' She was both furious and delighted. At twelve, she had not yet lost the childish capacity to be simultaneously angry and amused at some parental caprice. Her mouth was set but her eyes sparkled.

Thomas shrugged again, arms still crossed, face still a mask of impish self-satisfaction. Gemma bashed his arm playfully with the flat of one hand, hard enough to demonstrate that there was some genuine irritation beneath a gesture which could also be interpreted affectionately. Thomas bashed her arm back in the same spirit.

Edith watched them and felt secure. She and Gemma never had to engage in such ambivalent horseplay, the shoutings and gentle thumpings which showed that daughter and father loved each other to distraction while also driving each other mad. Things were straightforward for mothers. Thomas, she knew, was going to have a much more complex time.

She smiled indulgently at both of them.

Somehow, over the following year, the sands shifted. Edith realised only slowly what had happened. The simplicity of her love for Gemma was proving her undoing, for Gemma was no longer a simple child. She was growing away from herself, needing nothing, wanting everything.

It was gradual, the change. Gemma became more and more irritable with her mother, keener to be physically independent – to iron her own clothes, use a different shampoo. She stopped telling Edith about the things she had learnt or overheard at school, saving them up for when Thomas came home from work.

One day, just after she had arrived home, she came down the stairs to where Edith was cleaning the hallway skirting-board, stood over her and said, 'Mum, I've started a period.'

Edith sat back on her heels and gazed at her daughter. She hadn't got round to explaining about the monthlies yet. She had been meaning to for the past year, but Gemma was often tired and cross when she got home from school and Thomas was always around in the evenings or at the weekends. And now, here she was, all grown-up and matter-of-fact, not asking her mother but telling her, letting her know.

'Oh,' Edith said, helplessly, pulling off her rubber gloves. 'I'd better get you something.'

'It's all right,' said Gemma. 'Claire at school gave me some Lil-lets. I'll need something for tonight, though, and tomorrow.'

Edith stood, hesitated, then went up the stairs to the bathroom. She frowned to herself. It's all right? A friend at school gave her something? Gemma shouldn't be using tampons at her age. She bent to the cupboard under the bathroom sink and removed the hair-dryer and curlers to find where her sanitary towels were hidden at the back, wrapped firmly in Boots bags. How had this happened without her daughter needing her?

All evening she watched Gemma for signs that she was feeling unwell or upset. She showed none. When Thomas came home, she was at the dining table with a mathematics exercise book.

'Dad?' she asked, without lifting her head, calling out to the hall where Thomas was removing his shoes. He came into the lounge.

'Mr Roberts showed us a slide-rule today. Did you have a slide-rule?'

It was later that year that Edith realised how completely she had lost her daughter, how far away from her she had moved.

Three was only just enough to play most of the board games. They were really designed for families of four. Even the ones that could be played by fewer took for ever that way, as if to emphasise the inadequacy of a pair or trio. They had had some interminable games of Scrabble.

When they took Gemma to the toy section at the back of Skeffington Furnishings, she spent ages with her head cocked to one side reading the instructions on the games, looking for one which would be suitable for her triangular family.

'Here!' she called over to them one afternoon, swivelling her head to where her parents waited patiently. 'This one!' She was holding Cluedo.

Thomas gave a peremptory nod of assent. Board games were good for mental development, he said. They stimulated logic.

At the till, while Thomas paid, Gemma came and put her arm round her mother's waist. It was a cheerful, unselfconscious gesture of the sort she rarely made any more.

'There are just enough of us, Mum,' she said, nodding towards the counter at the game.

'Yes,' said Edith, hugging her daughter round the shoulders, 'there are.'

That evening, a Saturday, they settled down for a game. Gemma and Thomas opened the box while Edith made coffee. When she came back into the dining room, holding the tray of drinks, they had unfolded the board and were sitting close together at the table, heads bent, examining the rule book. Gemma was saying, 'Dr Black has been found dead on Saturday evening at approximately 8.45 p.m. Foot of the stairs ... it's marked X.' She and her father both lifted their heads and examined the board, where a white X marked the spot.

'Mum, here, you've got to look,' Gemma said, as Edith put the tray down on the dining table and turned to the sideboard for coasters.

'I'm looking,' she replied, over her shoulder.

'Cause of death has yet to be determined.' Gemma picked up a small plastic bag from the red carton inside the box. She opened it and tipped the contents onto the table. The murder weapons tinkled as they tumbled out. There was a tiny golden candlestick, a tiny dagger, an inch-long spanner and a miniature revolver, a little iron bar with a kink in it and a short length of bright yellow cotton knotted in a noose.

'That's the rope,' said Gemma, pointing at it. 'It was found in . . . the ballroom.'

Edith sat down. 'You mean they couldn't tell whether he was shot, strangled, stabbed or hit over the head?'

'*Mum*,' said Gemma, dropping her shoulders ostentatiously and gritting her teeth, 'that's not the *point*.'

'That's not the point, Mum,' added Thomas. He was assembling the suspects, tiny plastic people who slotted into little coloured circles, so that they could stand upright on the board.

'Colonel Mustard, Professor Plum, Reverend Green, Mrs Peacock, Miss Scarlett and Mrs White,' Gemma declared, as her father placed them on the board. The figures were about the same height as the tiny golden candlestick. Edith imagined trying to kill somebody with a candlestick five feet six inches tall.

'We have to put a character, a weapon and a room card secretly into the envelope. I'll do it! I'll do it!' Gemma was shuffling the small packs of cards and selecting one from each, face down.

A lengthy debate then ensued about whether the remaining cards should be shuffled all together before they were dealt, or whether they should each receive an equal number of characters, weapons and rooms. Edith did not participate. When she eventually received her cards, she found she had been dealt Reverend Green and Miss Scarlett, the revolver, the study, billiard room and conservatory. 'So it could have been any of these?' she asked, holding up her cards.

'No, Mum,' Gemma said patiently. 'You know it's definitely *not* any of those. The answer is in the envelope. It's a process of elimination.' She tore a sheet of paper from a small pad and pushed it over to her mother. 'Here, you've got to make a note of everything. When you think you know you can accuse somebody, but only if you're sure. If you're wrong, you're out.'

'But an accusation isn't the same as a suggestion. Explain to her, Gemma,' Thomas waved a hand, then lifted his coffee to his lips.

'When you go into a room, say you're Mrs White and you go into the ballroom, you suggest who you think did it, like, Colonel Mustard with the candlestick. That's just a suggestion. Say I've got Colonel Mustard, I show him to you, so you know it's not him. But Dad doesn't know I've got him. I could be showing you the candlestick or the ballroom, but if he's got the ballroom and already knows that it was maybe the candlestick, he'll guess that I've got Colonel Mustard and cross him off his list. So it's not just you guessing when you've got your turn. You guess all the time.'

'So,' said Edith, pursing her lips, then un-pursing them, 'if I've got Miss Scarlett and Mrs White, say, I know it's not them, but what if I say Reverend Green and you don't show me anything. Does that mean he did it?'

Gemma paused.

'Not necessarily,' interjected Thomas. 'She might not have Reverend Green but she might have the lounge. If you said lounge, she would show you that and I wouldn't have to show you anything. I might have the Reverend Green sitting right here. I would only have to show you if she didn't have the lounge or the murder weapon. You don't know whether I've got it or not.'

'So how am I supposed to know?'

'You work it out, Mum,' Gemma said impatiently, picking up the dice. 'We'll be here all night,' she grumbled. 'We've got to shake to see who goes first.'

Thomas scored a six. He went first.

It soon became clear to Edith that she was very much out of her depth. She had imagined that any game involving logical deduction would be simply a matter of working your way through the various options, but it was rapidly apparent that Cluedo was not nearly as logical as it first appeared. Her piece was Professor Plum. For some reason, Thomas and Gemma both seemed convinced that Professor Plum might have done it and kept calling her into different rooms on the board to account for herself. One minute, she was in the hall, trying to eliminate the lead piping. The next, she would be summoned to the kitchen and it would be *suggested* that she might have seen off Dr Black with the spanner. Just as she had nipped out of the secret passage from the kitchen to the study, she would be spirited off to the billiard room to be plonked suggestively down next to the rope.

As far as Edith could tell, you had no control over your character or his or her whereabouts. Consequently, she couldn't give two hoots about Professor Plum and felt much more attached to the fates of Reverend Green and Miss Scarlett. They were innocent parties, she knew, because she held their cards in her hands, but they were still liable to be accused at any moment. What if she were to slip the cards between her knees? Would that save them or damn them? What if she were simply to lie when Thomas or Gemma demanded to know if she was clutching the revolver?

It was her turn. She nipped into the conservatory. 'Mrs

Peacock in the conservatory with the dagger,' she suggested, hopefully.

Thomas and Gemma let out a simultaneous groan. Gemma put her cards face down on the table and dropped her head into her hands. '*Mum!*'

'What?'

'You must *know* that it *can't* be the conservatory because you showed me that about half an hour ago and you've been on and on about the dagger, which I eliminated straight away because Dad's got it and I'm sure he's shown it to you by now and you're not being *logical*.'

'Gemma . . .' said Thomas.

'But she's not, Dad. What's the point of playing with someone who doesn't get it? It spoils the whole point of having three people.'

'I know,' said Thomas, 'but you've just spoiled it by giving away all that information. I didn't know your mother had the conservatory.'

'Well, *she*'s spoiled it already.'

Edith saw that Gemma was close to tears. It sometimes happened when the games went on too long. She was still young to be sitting up late.

Thomas had noticed too. He put his hand on top of Gemma's and leant towards her. 'I know, but you must remember that your mother doesn't really understand this sort of thing. It doesn't matter. We can still play.'

'I may not be very logical,' Edith said stiffly, raising her voice to get their attention, 'but I would say I do have some common sense, and this game has no sense to it at all as far as I can see.'

They both looked at her.

'Common *sense*,' Gemma muttered angrily.

Edith was about to reprimand her when Thomas jumped in. 'Common sense didn't help Dr Black much, did it, eh, Gemma?' He nudged her with his elbow, trying to chivvy her back to her normal cheerful mood. 'I'd say he was a pretty sensible sort of person, being a doctor and so on. Just look what happened to him.'

Gemma scraped at the side of her nose with a forefinger, a habit which she knew annoyed her mother. 'No,' she chortled. 'He still ended up at the bottom of the stairs with his head caved in or whatever. *Common sense* is no good to him now.'

She and Thomas grinned and shrugged, like a pair of conspiratorial monkeys.

Gemma picked her cards up and said, 'It's my go now. We'll skip Mum.' She was happy again.

Edith lowered her gaze back to her cards but she no longer focused on them. She was indeed superfluous as far as Thomas and Gemma's games were concerned. Perhaps the least she could do was not make a fool of herself.

She thought, my daughter is cruel. Gemma had acquired the casual unkindness of the older child, the blithe assumption that because mothers are always there and always providing, they need never be pleased or taken into account. How old would Gemma be when she realised that Edith would not always be there? Twenty? Thirty? Maybe it would not dawn on her until she had children of her own.

Edith thought, I might die before Gemma realises how precious and unique I am. She might never realise that I know how much she loves me.

I am not clever, she thought, not like Thomas or Gemma. I will never write a poem like the ones in those books that Gemma has started reading all the time – but I have done something else. I have given birth to a daughter, and she is a greater poem than anything you could find between the covers of a book. Her hair is shiny. Her limbs are long. She is strong, strong flesh and blood – and I did it. I made her.

All at once, she was filled with a desire to stand up and seize Gemma, to shake her out of sheer joy. I *made* you, she wanted to shout. My life has not been wasted. Just look what I have done.

Thomas was showing Gemma a card, winking at his daughter knowledgeably. Neither of them looked at Edith. They never do, she thought.

Murder was not something to be afraid of in Rutland, unlike the rest of the country where it seemed as contagious as chicken pox. Thomas took the newspaper to work with him each morning but Edith often had a chance to glance through it when she came down to put the kettle on. She would pick it up from where it had flopped and fluttered onto the mat, then scan the headlines as she walked into the kitchen. If there was anything interesting to read, she would lie it flat on the countertop and look at it as she lifted the caddy and teapot from the shelf.

The stranger in the alleyway – those stories were always irresistible. What did the victims think as they went under? *If only*. If only they hadn't gone out that night to post the letter, visit the pub, meet a friend. If only their aunt hadn't telephoned just before they left – they would have been safely through the alleyway before the stranger had arrived there. If only they hadn't decided to take the short cut because they were late.

What were the chances of something like that happening? A million to one? Was it less likely than winning the lottery?

There were no alleyways in Nether Bowston. Thomas was keen on security, all the same. He became even more keen after he was made redundant. That was a bad time for all of them. It took Edith some months to realise just how bad. He seemed so cheerful and resolute at first, buying a fax machine and getting some headed paper printed. He never explained later why his ideas for starting a business didn't bear fruit. All he said was 'People don't appreciate good managerial skills these days.'

Instead, he managed the house. He fitted window locks. He took over the housekeeping. He told her in which areas they would have to economise.

The one thing he was not prepared to economise on was Gemma's schooling. That, at least, was sacrosanct.

When Edith saw how poor Gemma's exam results were, she went upstairs to the bathroom and locked the door, hiding herself away from all the pain and silence which she knew would be washing around downstairs. It was as if the house was being flooded. The disappointment would be knee-high already.

The worst of it was, she had known all along. She had accompanied Thomas to parents' evenings at the school and sat in silence while he grilled the teachers about Gemma's prospects. While he talked, lectured them, she had watched the teachers' faces, seen how they had acquired the stiff, careful expressions of diplomats. Gemma had never been top of the class, although she had always done well in English. Thomas seemed to think that if they pushed facts into her it would fill her up with knowledge, as a postman's van was filled with sacks of letters which could be simply poured out when they were required. With each revision session Thomas subjected Gemma to, Edith watched her daughter's academic prospects recede. In the run-up to Gemma's exams she had walked around the house thinking, let me be wrong, for once, let me be wrong.

She sat on the edge of the bath and rested her hands on both knees, leaning her weight forward and rocking slightly. She watched the marbled pattern of the lino and thought, I will never be as helpless as I am now.

Gemma seemed to take things quite well, all things considered. She stayed in her room a lot, reading. On several occasions, Edith wondered whether she should go up there and sit on the end of her bed and talk to her, the way she used to when Gemma had the 'flu, but she didn't know how to begin talking about Gemma's future. Thomas would come up with something.

They decided that there was no point in Gemma going back to that school. At one point, Thomas said he was seriously considering suing them for all the money they had taken over the years. Gemma would have been better off at home, he said. He could have done a better job than that lot.

Edith had to admit that it was nice having her daughter around during the day, being able to care for her in the way they had done when she was a toddler. She could make sure she got a proper lunch, for one thing.

Quite often, Gemma seemed tired and listless in the afternoons, slumped in an easy chair with her feet over one arm, turning the pages of one of her books slowly. Edith would sit in an opposite chair reading a magazine and say gently, across the room, 'Why don't you just fall asleep, dear? Take a little nap.' As the winter advanced, the house became hotter. Their central heating was always too hot or too cold. It was freezing in the evenings, so they usually went to bed early, but in the afternoons it could be baking. What could be nicer, after a warm bowl of soup at lunchtime, than to fall asleep in an easy chair?

It wasn't until January that Edith began to worry about Gemma's future. The arrival of the New Year seemed to imply a fresh start. On the morning of January 1st, Thomas went round the breakfast table asking them both what their resolutions were. Edith said what she said every year: to lose some weight, take more exercise and learn a foreign language. Thomas said he was going to re-do the guttering, and enjoy himself more, now he didn't have so many responsibilities. Gemma said she couldn't think of anything.

As she bowed her head back down over her cereal, Edith met Thomas's gaze. The look on his face was one of weary puzzlement. Edith gave a small shrug. Thomas looked back at his daughter with a half-smile of sadness and indulgence.

He is a kind man, Edith thought, for all his silly insistences and the way he gets worried about money all the time. He wants the best for our daughter and has done everything within his power to make sure she gets it. I could have done a lot worse than Thomas Cowper.

They took the local paper every Friday. It was in March that Thomas came through to the kitchen one morning waving it and saying. 'Good job I fitted those window locks. Look at this.'

The front-page story was headed BURGLARY EPIDEMIC – NO HOME IS SAFE. It was written by their Chief Reporter. Edith leant over, clutching a box of Weetabix, and glanced through the story. 'Seems to be mostly in Oakham,' she said.

Thomas shook his head vigorously, 'No no no, in here, inside, they've done a special report. They've got someone from nearly every village talking about something that's happened recently.'

He laid the paper flat on the counter top.

The *Record* had done a centre-fold which showed a map of Rutland with the villages and main roads marked. Each village had a line attached which drew the eye to a small boxed paragraph at the side. Inside the box, recent crimes were listed. Nether Bowston's box said:

26th Feb – attempted break-in Parson's Lane
2nd March – bicycle stolen in High Road
14th March – village postbox vandalised

'How do you vandalise a postbox?' Edith murmured sceptically.

'Edith,' Thomas said sternly, 'this is no joking matter, you know. Think about Gemma.'

'Well, I am,' Edith replied. 'But I don't think it's right them doing that. It might frighten the old people.'

'Maybe they've got a reason to be frightened.'

Thomas scooped up the paper and left the room.

An hour later, Gemma came into the kitchen and said, 'Mum, what's Dad doing?'

'I don't know,' said Edith. She was wringing out a J-cloth. 'What is he doing?'

'He just came into my room and checked the window and took the key. He didn't knock or anything.'

Thomas bustled in. He was carrying a small biscuit tin which clattered metallically. He brushed past them to the window and leant to reach the ledge, where the keys were hidden under a flower pot. He extracted them, prised open the tin's lid and dropped them in. Then he bustled out again.

'But how am I going to open my window when it's hot?' asked Gemma, her voice a childish wail.

Edith sighed. 'Oh, I'm sure he'll put them all somewhere.' She turned back to the sink.

The man in the shop knew all about the bicycle theft. He told Edith about it a fortnight or so after the *Record*'s special report.

'Easy pickings,' he said.

She had hurried down to get there just before it closed at six o'clock. She had flung a coat on but it had proved a mistake. The weather had become suddenly warm and she felt a flush of sweat as she pushed the shop door open.

The shop had changed hands the previous year and Edith did not know what The Man in the Shop was called, although they conversed every time she went in. Her ignorance embarrassed her.

She was handing him a sliced loaf and a see-through bag of small, rock-hard tomatoes which she had picked from his tiny selection of fresh fruit 'n' veg.

'Round here,' The Man in the Shop said congenially as he weighed the tomatoes, 'there's old folk who still don't lock their doors and they know it, you know. That's why they come out from Leicester. And Birmingham. They come all the way from Birmingham. The Indians don't come – they'd stick out like a sore thumb. But the others do.'

'We used to live in Leicester,' said Edith, conversationally.

The direction of his speech did not bend to her remark. 'They come out in the afternoons. I've seen them. They think people will be at work. If they can't get in anywhere they just smash things, just for the hell of it. I had this bloke came in last month for two pints of milk. He had one of those yellow helmets on and things on his elbows and knees. He was on holiday. Tall, skinny and a beard. He went outside and was back in two ticks saying, my bike's gone. He'd just propped it outside for two ticks thinking, village like this, no one around. I told him, you can't do that round here. You never know when they're going to crawl out of the woodwork. Easy pickings.'

Edith left the shop with the bread and tomatoes in a skinny blue bag. As she walked home she glanced at the surrounding bushes, half expecting to see the feathered and painted face of a Red Indian lurking, even though they weren't called Red Indians any more.

It was true. The village was always deserted.

She had been to a Bring and Buy at the Village Hall last year and had seen a display on a stall run by local Brownies. It was called Victorian Nether Bowston. Enlarged copies of sepia photos were pinned to the stall showing the village as it was 'In Olden Times'. The Brownies were all dressed up as mini housemaids, apart from one who wore cut-off raggedy trousers and had a dirty face. 'I'm a sweep,' she was announcing to anyone who passed the stall. 'They send me up chimneys.'

Edith had paused to look at the photos. The tiny High Road was virtually unchanged, curving round the green, lined by the squat little cottages with their small square windows and squat little doors.

What surprised her was the people. The street was full of people. There were three shops, including an open-fronted one which might have been a blacksmith's. A group of four women stood in front of it, a horse and cart beside them. Two men were sitting on a stone step nearby. Another woman with three children was approaching them. It was a busy village street.

Edith thought about that picture sometimes, on her quiet walks back from the shop. A solitary car might sweep huskily past, but there was never anyone else on foot. Her feet would clatter on the path, the sound large and echoey in the still air. The windows of most of the cottages were so small that she never saw anyone moving inside them. The whole of Nether Bowston might be deserted.

It seemed odd to think that a village as silent as theirs could ever have bustled in the way that old photo had implied. Nobody worked in the villages any more, they all went elsewhere in cars, but there were other people around; old people, women with young children. Why did nobody come out any more? Why did everybody stay inside?

There was the cat. Edith didn't know who it belonged to but it often lazed or slunk about the village green. It was a furry ginger tom, its long hair scruffy with fluffballs and bits of undergrowth. Sometimes it would sit on the verge and watch her as she passed. When it miaowed, its face scrunched up and its pointed yellow teeth were exposed. Most cats miaowed vowel sounds, but this one made a harsh, tiny consonant, an *ich*. She thought of it as the Nazi cat.

She saw it that evening. It was sitting on the path in front of her as she rounded the corner into their lane. It didn't move as she approached. It was facing her, its gaze lifted, unimpressed.

She didn't like to step over it, it was such a mangy thing, so she moved out into the road and walked round it.

At her gateway, she hesitated, looking towards their house. It, too, looked empty from the outside. How strange.

She closed the five-barred gate behind her. Now it was hot again, the creosoted surface of the gate felt slighty sticky. Her feet swooshed on the stones as she turned. They had put the gravel down when Gemma was small, so that she wouldn't be able to whizz down the drive on her tricycle and out into the road. Thomas had talked of replacing it with tarmac one day, but then he had pointed out that it was actually a good security device. From inside the house, you could hear the crunch of anyone approaching the front door.

Edith crunched up the drive, her shoes digging and scuffing. Halfway up, she stopped, put down the plastic bag and removed her coat, slinging it over one arm. It was so sticky and unpleasant that she couldn't even bear to wait until she reached her own front door. It was ludicrously hot for April, particularly when it wasn't even sunny. It wasn't natural.

She thought this thought, *unnatural*, as she lifted her key. Then, momentarily, all thought was stopped.

The door swung open. She took half a step forward, before being arrested by the sight of her daughter. Gradually, and instantly, Edith Cowper's gaze gathered together what she could see.

Gemma was frozen against the wall, standing straight but giving the hunched, tied-up impression of being in a crouched position. She was wide-eyed, her pupils as fathomless as black holes. Her right eyebrow was matted with blood. Blood was speckled on other parts of her face in tiny artistic dots and a smeared streak of blood ran down her arm. As Gemma turned her body, slowly, it seemed, to face her, Edith saw more blood on the front of Gemma's lemon-coloured t-shirt.

She had one additional slow moment in which to think, my daughter is hurt, and to feel herself tipping towards her.

At the same time, she felt a slam in the lower chest, as if she had been hit with a wide, flat object which was at once hard and immeasurably soft – and then her daughter was very close to her, almost supporting her as she pitched forward, and she caught a glimpse of Gemma's ever-widening gaze, a gaze so hollow and frightened that she seemed scarcely human.

She fell on her side and rolled onto her back, a hand lifted instinctively, for now there could be no mistake. Her daughter had one arm raised high and the black point of the knife was a dark star descending.

Her thoughts were everything and nothing. She knew she was about to die. At the same time the fear and panic were so all-consuming that there was hardly space in which to be aware of anything. The shock of it condensed thought.

I am being killed. My daughter is killing me. I am becoming a murder. The fact of my death will be wholly obscured by its manner. I am now a murder victim, devoid of personality or history. I will never have the chance to become anything else.

There was no time to identify these ideas or separate them from one another before she lost consciousness. She was hardly aware of the second blow. A darkness was gathering over her and only one thought surfaced clearly: how lonely I am.

9

The genesis of a moral dilemma lies not in the choice between right
or wrong but in the recognition that choice itself is possible.

Hamlyn Wilkes
A Murderous Heart

*I*t's hell trying to get a parking place in the centre of
Oakham on a Saturday. It's because of the market. By
mid-afternoon, the stalls are beginning to pack up and things
are quietening down.

As I drove by that Saturday, I heard the tinkle of bells,
a whoop and clatter. The Morris Men were performing by
the butter cross. They were touring the county as part of
the Independence celebrations – that kind of thing would be
happening all summer. Peter, our Chief Sub, was also our
Picture Editor and he was supposed to be following them
round getting some good stuff for next week. I hoped he
had remembered, what with all the excitement about Doug.
I nearly stopped to check he was there. I had to remind
myself I was on a mission.

It was such a normal day, that day. I couldn't believe that
I was doing anything out of the ordinary.

I parked on Stamford Road, a few yards round the bend,
pulling onto the verge so that I wouldn't get clouted by some
idiot driver swinging out of town.

Outside the library a small, tweedy man was handing out
leaflets for the Referendum Party. I took one as I passed, folding it and stuffing it in my pocket. I couldn't get excited about
the election. Rutland was as safe as houses for the Tories.

Oakham library is a modern brick bungalow with large windows and an air of sleepy helpfulness. I used to borrow science fiction from it when I was an adolescent, running my fingers along the metal shelving looking for the familiar yellow hardbacks. I tried other types of novel once or twice but the yellow hardbacks were my favourite. I was guaranteed a story. When I had grazed through all they had, I stopped going. It never occurred to me that I could order more.

It was always quiet. Even on a Saturday, there were only a few other people around: an elderly lady by the large print books and a couple of kids squeaking softly in the children's section. The Ordnance Survey maps were on a stand by the information desk. It would have been quicker to ask for help but I didn't want to draw attention to myself. Eventually, I found the right ones, No. 130 for Grantham and No. 141 for Kettering and Corby.

Burley Wood was dissected, half on each map. There wasn't much detail but I could see a series of criss-cross paths coming to a central point in the middle of the wood. There were no other obvious landmarks. Ashpit Spinney was a small stain to the right, as if the printer's ink had blotted. No paths were marked.

Altogether, it was the biggest wooded area in Rutland, several hundred acres, but on the map it still looked small – the pale green spread of it dwarfed by the curving blue of Rutland Water. Thirty coppers could cover that in a couple of days, I thought, shaking my head. Ashpit Spinney was tiny. I could cover that myself in under an hour.

Outside the library, the Referendum man handed me another leaflet. It joined the first one in my pocket.

As I turned towards the car, I saw David Poe. He was standing on the kerb at the top of Burley Road, waiting to cross. He hadn't seen me. I scurried down Stamford Road.

As I drove out of Oakham, I felt freedom wash over me, a feeling as real and as fresh as a sudden summer rainstorm. I always feel like that as I pull out into the countryside along that road, no matter how many times I've done it. I've noticed other drivers picking up speed with the same alacrity. Maybe it is the wide swoop of the vista ahead; the fields, the air, the water.

I had a long chat with Lizzie once, about men. She said the best bit about sleeping with a man was getting up at his place the following morning, getting into your car and leaving – driving away thinking, I've done that, now I'm off. At the time I thought, better not to do it in the first place, maybe, and I think I said as much. Later I realised I was envious. I didn't want to sleep around like her – but that feeling of leaving, that was what appealed to me. I suppose that is why Andrew lives the way he does. He gets the feeling of leaving all the time.

I wondered whether he would still be there when I got back. I doubted it. I couldn't think of anything more likely to put him on the highway with his thumb raised than an unexpected visit from our mother.

As I drove up the hill, I thought about Doug lying on his back in Leicester Royal Infirmary, helpless and ill, on such a lovely sunny day.

I parked more carefully than on my previous visit, pulling the car up to the five-barred gate where it would be partially hidden by the overgrown bushes that sprouted either side. Drivers coming over the brow of the hill would glimpse it as they passed, but it was much less noticeable than before.

I've never been that interested in exploring. It isn't in my blood. When you come from generations who have grown up in the countryside you think it is for working, not walking. One of our receptionists is a fully paid-up member of the Ramblers' Association. What *is* rambling, precisely? I wanted to ask her when she tried to sign me up. I understand what walking is – it is an action of the legs for the purpose of getting from A to B. But *rambling*? See you later, dear, I'm just going to ramble down to the post office.

In the field beyond the Spinney, a sparrowhawk was hovering. I watched as it swooped for a fieldmouse hidden in the undergrowth. Over the rise came the broken *ma-are* of sheep.

There was the stillness that the countryside acquires in sunlight. It is most noticeable in high summer but even then I could feel it – a heaviness, a thickness in the air. Einstein said that sunlight hit the earth at two kilograms per second. $E = mc^2$, one of the few things I can remember from General Science. If mass has energy, then I suppose energy must have mass, but it's still a funny way of putting it. It makes it sound as if Einstein thought that sunlight landed on the earth like a bag of sugar dropped from outer space.

There was a half-hearted twirl of barbed wire hanging from the top bar of the gate but it was old and loose. I eased it to one side. I glanced around, then clambered over, jumping down clumsily. I stepped round the bushes, out of sight, then paused to look at my hands. Then I set off down the track.

The edges of the wood were raggedy – the density would come later. For the first fifty yards it was like walking through nature's rubbish tip: nettles, dock leaves, dandelions ran wild. Elders twisted towards the sky.

I have a gardener's suspicion of elders. They aren't trees at all really, just big weeds. The seedlings sprout the minute they hit the soil. Their roots spread deep beneath the ground. They will take over, if you let them.

There were two of them at the back of my garden when I bought the cottage. I had to get some blokes in to deal with them. There is a superstition that you never speak ill of an elder in its presence. 'So,' the head bloke said to me quietly, regarding the bigger of the two. 'Shall we attend to this one first?' I nodded. 'Attend' meant chop down and poison the stump, but neither of us was going to say it out loud.

Nobody had attended to the elders in Ashpit Spinney. They had taken over. I thought ill of them as I passed.

It looked as though somebody had made the effort to plant a few conifers. A few yards of polite woodland lined the track, the sort of woodland that ramblers like to ramble in, with a heavy canopy and enough undergrowth to house a few rare invertebrates. I made a small, cynical grimace, remembering that I once bought a pair of earrings from a market in Birmingham which had a label attached reading *Genuine Wood*.

Further into the Spinney, it looked less genuine but more authentic, an untidy mixture of oak and maple, with one or two pale, feminine ash. The canopy was less dense underneath the ash trees. Einstein's sugar bags of sunlight broke through and plummeted down onto heaps of sedge and old bracken twisted around the floury tree trunks. There was the musty, broken scent of soil, dead wood, dying insect life. I knew that smell. I had a different version, a more rotten version, in my cottage. This was milder, diluted by the occasional breeze.

The track ended. Ahead, through the undergrowth, there was a small, scuffed path. The trees became denser, but I could just see that, at the far end of the path, there was a clearing.

I don't know how long that walk took. The path was narrow. It seemed to stretch and lengthen itself as I progressed along it. As I neared the clearing, the bushes closed in. Hard twigs poked at me. I ducked and dived as I walked. I began to feel like someone dreaming. The ground was uneven, coated with leaves and pine needles which had fallen, become soggy, then hardened. As I broke through into the clearing, I stumbled.

The clearing was oblong, with a huge fallen oak on one side which looked as though it had been coppiced once, then left derelict. After a few years, it must have become top heavy, then blown over. The trunk now lay on the ground with new branches sprouting vigorously along its length. I was close to the stool end, which bulged as high as my face, a spaghetti tangle of dead roots in yellow, grey and white. Soil and spiders' webs hung from the roots, a perfect home for lice and millipedes. It was a whole eco-system, a town like Oakham.

Beyond the clearing, I could see that the trees began to thin out again. The open fields would not be far away. I had walked the length of the Spinney.

It was a warm, still day but among the trees there was a movement of air, a shifting. Although the woods were silent, I could sense the scurrying of small things in the undergrowth around me.

I stood very still. A pigeon cooed precisely; two long calls followed by one short, three times in succession. I wondered what that meant in Morse. Pat and I learnt Morse code at school, during a brief sojourn in the Girl Guides. We also taught ourselves semaphore, a consequence of reading too much Arthur Ransome. We used to stand on opposite sides of the street waving our arms, signing to each other, *meet you in five mins outside the chippy*.

Then, I heard the flies. They must have been there all the time, but, as I stood, the noise they were making faded up in the echoey silence which followed the pigeon's call.

The sound of a large group of flies is both constant and various – a light buzzing punctuated by drilling noises which melt and move in the same way that the blackness of them weakens and intensifies if you watch them swarm.

It was only later, much later, that I realised why it took me a moment or two to hear the sound and acknowledge its implications. Over winter, we forget the noise that a swarm of flies can make. It is a summer noise, but one of such ubiquity that when we hear it again, we forget we had forgotten it.

I remembered, then forgot I was remembering. I thought, it's too early for flies. The warm weather must have brought them out.

The sound was making shapes above me. I turned and looked up.

She must have clambered along the trunk of the fallen oak, then climbed up onto the branches of the other tree from there. It was a lime tree, I think. The leaves were a youthful green.

One leg of the trousers was tied round a branch in a solid double knot. They were navy blue. She had wrapped the crotch round her neck, then tied the other leg. It was a thorough, determined job. She was still wearing her socks and trainers. A long yellow t-shirt hung down to her hips. It was smeared with brown stains, old blood and dirt. Her legs were bare but scratched and streaked with fluid. Flies clung to the fluid.

She was in profile. Her long hair covered most of her face but I could just see her half-open mouth.

The flies were all over her, her arms, her hair. They dripped from one leg, dancing away, returning. The noise of them deepened in my ears with the insistence of a dentist's implement until it felt as though they were inside my head.

Then, one of her legs twitched.

As I parked the car, haphazardly, outside my house, I realised that I was talking to myself, babbling out loud. 'So if we pull the photofit,' I was saying, 'can we bring the picture of the house backwards maybe and run the portrait shots on page one I think the portraits would look good do you know that Skeffington's are only going to run their ads until the end of July they gave us lots of notice that was nice but they say it's not economical Linda is going to write to them I think . . .'

I stopped. I tried to breathe calmly. My chest rose and fell at a normal rate but the air inside it felt thin, as if I was at altitude.

My legs shook as I walked the few feet to the front door. I almost fell upon it. I had forgotten that my mother might be there. I just wanted Andrew.

My brother was sitting on the bottom step of my stairs, smoking. Next to him was his Guatemalan bag. He was wearing a hat with matching embroidery. He had changed his t-shirt.

I stopped in the doorway. He twisted the stub of his cigarette against my banister, looked at me and said. 'Relax. She's gone.'

I moved into the room and folded down onto the sofa.

He stood and picked up his bag. 'I'm off,' he said. 'I need some money. Have you got any?'

I looked at him, unable to translate the expression on his face. I waved a hand over my bag, beside me on the sofa. He had never asked to borrow money from me before.

He strode over to the bag and picked it up.

'Andrew . . .' I said. My voice was weak and strained.

He wasn't looking at me. He was picking through my purse.

'There's forty pounds in here. I'm taking twenty. Fair enough, don't you think? After all, you owe me fifteen hundred. More, counting interest.'

I looked up at him. 'What are you *talking* about?' It was a shout but my voice was feeble. It came out hoarsely.

He looked down at me. 'Gran's money,' he said calmly. 'Mum told me about it. She told me a lot of other things as well. Mostly rubbish, of course – you know what she's like.'

'What did she say?' A sense of unreality had come over me. I couldn't believe we were discussing our mother.

'After I left. Gran's money. It had been in the building society all those years and we were going to get half each when you turned eighteen. I'd gone. Mum gave it all to you, to help you buy this place. Her latest idea is that you persuaded me to leave so that you would get all the money.'

'She's mad.'

'I know she's mad. I told her. That's not the point.'

I pushed myself up until I was facing him. My voice was broken. 'Andrew, please, for God's sake. I don't know what you're going on about.'

He had two ten-pound notes in his hand. He held them up, close to my face. 'In all these years, all the times I've come here, it never occurred to you to mention it? You didn't think maybe you could've asked if it was all right, just once?'

I lifted a hand, then dropped it. 'Oh, for God's sake you've always . . . You don't . . .'

He reached out and grabbed me. His fingers dug into my upper arms, the banknotes crumpled in his grasp. 'Don't *what*?' he spat, his voice harsh and bitter. 'Don't need money? Don't need to eat, maybe? Don't like clothes or CDs or buying a pint occasionally?' He gave me a single shake, a short, hard gesture of fury. His face was twisted. His voice became low, sibilant. 'I wouldn't mind, Alison, but it's bloody typical. You don't care about anyone. You're worse than Mum. At least she's bloody mad. You don't have any excuse. You just live here in this stupid little house because you're too bloody lazy and self-satisfied to do anything else. You think you're the big shot and you've no bloody idea. No ambition, nothing. You're *worse*. You've never asked me anything about what happened. Haven't you got any fucking curiosity?'

He released me. I sank back down on the sofa. He turned and picked up his bag.

At the door, he hesitated. I thought he was finally going to ask me if I was all right. Instead he said, 'Hope you had fun shopping.'

After a while, I ran a bath, filling it so full that I had to ease myself down gently in case the water overflowed. Lumps of foam as big as brains swung on the surface as I sank.

Steam filled the room. The window was open and the air that drifted in was a pleasant contrast to the sauna hovering over me. I lay with my head tipped back against the hard enamel, vaguely aware of the novelty of bathing mid-day. The sunlight made calming golden shapes against the wall.

My phone rang but I didn't move. My answer machine had broken down a month before and I hadn't got round to replacing it. Once I had realised I could manage without one, I found it liberating. The phone stopped, then rang again – obviously somebody found it difficult to believe that in this day and age some people don't have answer machines.

I did nothing.

I washed my hair in the bath. Normally I blow-dry it but I let it drip as I got dressed, combed it through, let it drip some more. I made myself a mug of hot, sweet tea. Later, I made a sandwich and left it uneaten on the kitchen table. I went to the phone and dialled 1471 and a mechanical woman told me that she did not have the caller's number. I sat on the settee for a time.

I went outside to the garden but decided I didn't want to sit out there. I came back inside. I found the sandwich on the kitchen table and tested it with a finger. The edges of the bread had become stiff and dry. I threw it away. I made another one, which I ate.

I went and lay down on the settee. I did nothing.

Sunday arrived. The phone rang once and I ignored it again. Then I thought it might be David, so I rang the Stag Hotel. They told me he had checked out on Saturday morning. He had gone back to London.

After I had put the phone down, I became aware of a fat

bluebottle zig-zagging lazily across the sitting room. I went outside, to the garden.

For all of Sunday, I did nothing.

I was first to arrive at the office on Monday morning. I sat at my desk, looking at how neat and tidy it was, noticing as if for the first time how well organised I am.

Cheryl was late. When she arrived, she seemed tired. Doug was back home already. He had discharged himself over the weekend. She had been to see him that morning. I told her I would go round at lunchtime and she looked at me.

'Just to see how he is,' I said.

The others came in gradually. Everyone was quiet. Doug's absence was apparent in a way that it hadn't been on Friday, as if the drama of his being rushed to hospital had somehow obscured the truth of his illness. The office felt empty.

Cheryl and I discussed what to do with that week's issue. I told her she should write up her background notes on the Cowpers. I said I would do the other stuff – the Village Correspondents, the letters page. She looked surprised that I was relinquishing the big story. We didn't talk about my call from George Bloomfield, not with the others around, but the fact of it stood between us as real and as tangible as if someone had erected a bullet-proof screen between our desks.

I worked on a story about the high number of badger deaths in Rutland. Rabbits get killed because they shoot recklessly across the road. Badgers die because they amble benignly in the verges.

Halfway through it, my head began to feel hazy. I went to the Ladies and gagged over the toilet bowl. Then I went back to the badgers.

As I left the office, around noon, I thought, maybe I should talk to Doug. He was so solid, and his solidity now seemed to imply a moral grasp of the world around him. What would he do? What would he have done?

I walked to the far end of the quiet High Street and over the railway line to the part of town that some people refer to as 'the wrong side of the level crossing' – the side of town with the council estates and local comprehensive, the side of town where I grew up.

Doug's bungalow was only three streets from my parents' house but I had never visited before.

It was a long time before he answered the door. When he did, he looked at me as if he had no feelings either way about my turning up.

He took the flowers I had bought and put them on the dining table in front of the window, then moved with great care to a nearby winged armchair, gesturing me to take the one opposite.

His sitting room reeked of bachelorhood; the sad, middle-aged sort. On top of the television, there was a photograph of him and his late wife, an anniversary or some similar event. The silver frame was tarnished. Behind every eccentric, there is this backdrop, I thought; the woolly curtains that have never been washed, the gas fire. Scratch any *bon viveur* and you come up with a man who hasn't weighed himself for years because the idea of standing his loose white flesh on a pair of scales makes him want to burst into tears.

I offered to make us both a cup of tea but he clearly wasn't interested. He sank slowly into his chair. Once he was in it, he looked as though he would never move, as if he was a giant mould which had grown there. He stared at me keenly, across the eight feet or so that separated us. I was perched on the edge of my chair like a butterfly.

'So,' he said, after a pause, 'what's happening? Cheryl said everything's fine. I could tell just by looking at her. So come on then.'

I was caught off guard by his directness. 'Nothing. Nothing's happened,' I said. 'I've had a call from George Bloomfield, over the weekend. He wants to meet me tomorrow.' I paused. 'He didn't say what about.'

He exhaled heavily. 'Not wasting any time, are they?' His voice was thick with bitterness. 'I asked Cheryl if she'd spoken to them and she wouldn't say.'

'He's really pleased with what we've done on the Cowper story,' I said. 'He thought we'd done a really good job.'

'We did.'

I was surprised by his belligerence. I think I had imagined he would be more generous – the show must go on, and all that. I think I thought he might even wish me well.

'It's up to you, isn't it?' I said, softly. 'It's up to you whether or not you feel well enough and want to carry on.'

He stared at me. His eyes were grey and round. They had that rabbit-pinkness around the lids that everyone seems to acquire in late middle age. There was a moistness about Doug, I realised, which his illness had made obvious. I knew it should excite pity, but all I felt was disgust: and as I realised I was disgusted by him, I felt thrilled. This man had been my boss for eight years. I had worked for him since I left school; secretary, trainee reporter, assistant reporter . . . And now, in my mid-twenties, I was going to be offered an opportunity that had taken him another decade of hard, underpaid slog to achieve. In his day, promotion was a stony, laborious business – and here I was, leaping ahead.

Eventually he said, still staring at me, 'I knew you were an ambitious young lady.' He spoke slowly, with great deliberation. His heavy face remained still. The eyes continued to stare. 'That's why I hired you in the first place . . .' He stopped.

We sat in silence for a long time. Eventually, I shifted my gaze and contented myself with looking over his shoulder, to where my inappropriate daffodils sat wrapped in blush-coloured paper on his dining table, bathed in milky, filtered light.

I was turning the corner into the market square when I heard the sirens, a distant discordance of two or three. It took a moment or two for the sound of them to register – and in that moment, Cheryl came stomping from the office, bangles clinking. She slammed the door behind her. 'Come on,' she snapped, without greeting me. 'We can take my car.'

The police cars shot past as we were getting into her muddy Escort. Inside, it smelt of soil and cigarettes and dogs. She was talking as she started the engine. 'I think a whole load of stuff is up there already,' she said. 'I heard all these vehicles going past and I thought, it's busy for a Monday. There were vans. I saw the tail end of one as I stuck my head out the window.'

We had to wait at the pedestrian lights while an elderly lady tottered across the road. She paused halfway to lift a hand in gratitude. Cheryl lifted a hand in return. The police cars were out of sight.

'Where?' I said. 'Up where?'

'Could be Rutland Water,' she said, taking off in second gear and driving straight over the mini-roundabout, 'but the divers finished there middle of last week. At a guess, I'd say Burley Woods.'

We were pulling out of town before she asked me, 'What did Doug have to say?'

'He's fine,' I said carefully. I thought she might pursue it but she was staring up at the road ahead. The adrenalin of a story had gripped her. You're no different from the rest of us, I thought briefly.

As we came to the top of the hill, I saw two vans parked in the stony lay-by and four police cars ranged beside them. We pulled onto the verge. Inspector Collins was remonstrating with two officers who were standing by their car. He gestured over to us and raised his hands.

We hadn't got more than a yard from Cheryl's car when he came forward.

'Cheryl, Alison, look I'll phone you the minute we have anything. Just go back.'

'You must be joking,' Cheryl replied. 'Your boys woke the whole town up, John.'

He was already turning away, trotting back to where the gathering of officers was waiting. 'Just stay by the car, will you?' he shouted over his shoulder, flapping one hand at us and beckoning with the other to an officer in dark overalls who stood beside a van.

The officer in overalls opened the back doors of the van and there was loud, rusty barking. Two more officers jumped down, each accompanied by a dark brown Alsatian. Both of them held the dogs on tight leads but the animals still strained this way and that, their large heads dipping anxiously, paws scrabbling the pebbles beneath them. The officers swayed as they turned the animals round and manoeuvred them towards the gate.

Four other men were ripping the gate from its hinges. Inspector Collins was gesturing into the Spinney. The men set off in pairs. John Collins waited and gave directions to another officer, who was organising the remaining men, then he turned and, taking the men and dogs with him, started down the track.

We were leaning against the car. 'Damn,' Cheryl said to me, sideways. 'Peter was in the loo, otherwise I'd've brought him. We could have got some great pictures.'

'Yes,' I said.

'The dogs,' she added. 'People love police dogs.'

They were out of sight but we could still hear the barking. The men left behind were calling to each other. From their cars came the fierce fizz and crackle of their radios.

*　　*　　*

The opening of the inquest was just in time for our deadline. We cleared the front page in preparation. The inquest on the parents had been opened and adjourned the week before. Seeing as the forensics left no room for doubt, the Coroner announced that he would combine evidence on all three deaths in one session. Amidst the habitual welter of bureaucracy, under the high, dark-beamed ceiling of Oakham Castle, the Cowper family were reunited.

Most of the press had left by then. The crime reporters had all gone back to London once they had covered the discovery of Gemma's body. It was no longer a big story for the nationals, just a collection of facts.

Some stringers stayed around, just in case any interesting details emerged. David Poe was there. I saw him come in after the proceedings had begun, and perch on the end of one of the extra benches laid out at the back of the court. He didn't look my way.

By then we already knew that the police had searched the Spinney after receiving an anonymous phone call. I wondered if it could have been him. Had he seen me that day by Oakham Library, followed me perhaps? More likely it was Tim Gordon, suddenly discovering he had an imagination after all. Maybe he told somebody else, after he spoke to me. Maybe it was him trying to ring me that weekend. It's possible that someone else stumbled upon the body, but I don't think the police would have bothered with the dogs if they were looking for a corpse. I think they thought they might find her alive.

The pathologist was a Dr Elliot from the Royal. The body showed signs of mild dehydration, he said. The eyes were slightly sunken, the skin dry and beginning to lose its elasticity. She was thin, which could indicate that she had not eaten for some days, although Gemma Cowper's body weight was known to have been on the low side anyway.

It all fitted in with her having been in the woods for some time before she committed suicide. There were knife marks on the lower arms which were consistent with having been self-inflicted, possibly in an attempt to reach an artery in the wrists. A kitchen knife was found in a plastic bag in the clearing, along with some school exercise books, an orange juice carton and an empty Weetabix packet. There was also a small transistor radio with run-down batteries, some books and a folded woman's overcoat. All items were believed to have come from the Cowper family home.

Dr Elliot was a short man with thinning hair and the air of someone who enjoyed his own competency. His voice was clipped. He spoke in whole sentences. It was impossible for him to pinpoint exactly how long she had been dead, although he would estimate something in the region of two, possibly three days. It took at least a day for a body left in the open to reach ambient temperature. There were, however, no signs of the onset of decomposition, such as mottling of the skin or prominent blood vessels.

While he was speaking, there was a great silence in the court. We all had our heads down, making notes. Cheryl had come with me because her shorthand was better than mine and she could get everything down verbatim.

It sounded as though Gemma had hanged herself on the Friday, late in the evening probably, while I was drinking vodka in David Poe's hotel room. Perhaps it happened as he rested his hand on my thigh. Or maybe it was later that night, while Andrew and I were watching Gene Hackman on the telly. Maybe despair and madness took a final grip at the prospect of another night alone in a scurrying wood, another night when no one came.

It's possible it was even later, as dawn broke on the Saturday, as the greyness grew enough for her to climb the trunk of the fallen oak. That is when the metabolism is at its lowest ebb, when hopelessness can become overwhelming. It must have been cold at that hour. She must have shivered as she removed her trousers and tied the knot.

It couldn't possibly have been any later than that and maybe it was earlier. She had probably been dead for some time before I found her.

A police inquiry was announced, to investigate why the woods were not searched earlier. 'Eggy faces,' John told me, off the record. He's in the clear at least. It wasn't his fault. If the fat super had listened to him, she would have been found alive at the beginning of the week.

He asked me not to run a piece on the inquiry until the results were released. In return, he would make sure the *Record* was the first to get the details. Cheryl thought it was unethical. She thought we should do a big splash on the way the search for Gemma had been handled, but in my new capacity as Acting Editor, I overruled her.

George Bloomfield was not exactly generous. He clearly thought I should be grateful for whatever I got. He didn't give me a full Editor's salary to start with – it wasn't much more than what I was getting as Chief Reporter. But he did promise me a decent increment when the position was confirmed.

In the weeks after the inquest, I worked in my garden. The evenings lengthened. I planned what I might do with the extra cash. I thought about building a terrace at the back, with a stone wall. It would take a lot of topsoil but I thought maybe I could fill in some of it with builder's rubble. I was only going to turf or seed it. It didn't matter how much rubbish was underneath.

I decided to sort out the damp in the kitchen. I got a bloke in who suggested putting up some two-and-a-half-millimetre polystyrene and pasting it with mould inhibitor. Warm air wouldn't condense on polystyrene, he said. If I painted it with mould inhibiting emulsion as well, it would look just like a normal kitchen. I would finally have walls which were white instead of a textured, glistening grey.

I did some sums and realised the roof would have to wait. So would the wiring.

The magnolia bloomed. It was late. It looked good, though. So did the white flowers on the plum tree. In my herb patch, I saw that the angelica had grown into a big green shrub while most of my other herbs had had it. How much angelica could I use?

The apple tree was my biggest problem. I sprayed it with lime sulphur twice a week for the rest of the spring, worrying about the prospect of another warmish, dampish summer. Then there were the woolly aphis. I had a chat with Miss Crabbe one evening, across the fence, and she suggested tar oil.

Miss Crabbe had earwigs in her dahlias. 'Night feeders, earwigs,' she said, nodding at her plants, and I had a sudden image of herds of the little beasts crawling out under the cover of darkness to munch their way through her borders.

Miss Crabbe and I became quite chummy. She gave me some slug poison, one part metaldehyde to three parts bran.

Sitting in the garden one evening, I remembered how Andrew and I were once digging over a patch and he held up his trowel and said, 'Look.' On the end of it, there were two centipedes, one slightly larger than the other. He pointed to the small one with a soiled finger and said, 'The lesser of two weevils.'

We think of murder as this huge big thing, a thing too large for our ordinary minds to encompass. But I know now how mundane it is – how it can happen and mean almost nothing. Our bodies are so frail, our skin so thin. So much of life is so much tougher; wood, metal, rope. Our flesh is almost liquid, after all. It's amazing we don't melt in the sun.

Insects are much more resourceful than we are. They have so many ways of surviving. Tortrix moths, for instance, feed on the foliage of roses. They fasten the leaves together with sticky cobwebs and you have to pick them off by hand. You can tell if it's a tortrix moth by poking it with a finger and shouting at it. When they are disturbed, they wriggle backwards.

She couldn't possibly have been alive when I saw her. The flies.

Epilogue

Somehow, over the summer, I lost my enthusiasm for the renovations I had planned. I never did tar-oil my apple tree, or get the polystyrene up in my kitchen.

I don't know what happened. Perhaps it was that rain in June. I stayed indoors a lot. I stopped listening to the news on the radio. Then I stopped listening to the radio at all. I drove to work each day in silence.

It has been one of the wettest, hottest summers ever – unpleasant for everybody, disastrous for the garden. Mildew flourishes in conditions like this.

The attic office is mine now. Cheryl left the *Record* in July, to work for a Stamford rival. I have a new deputy, a young man from Uppingham called Robert. He used to run a community press there, printing parish leaflets and so on. He's very thorough but he doesn't strike me as the kind of person who could nose out a good story. That takes imagination, after all. You have to find the root of it.

I understand now that, however momentous a story is, it begins when you first know of it. The Cowpers' murder began as I stood at my kitchen window one Friday morning, sipping tea, and heard the ambulance and police cars speeding quietly through the village. We all like to pretend that when we hear an ambulance our hearts quicken with sympathy for the person or people it is going to collect. What we really experience is a small thrill. We would like to follow it, if we could. It is hurtling towards a story.

I've been spending so much time at the office that I haven't really done anything else. Doug's filing system was a mess, and I wanted to re-structure the advertising department. You

171

have to do that kind of thing when you take over, to let people know you've arrived. I've been working in the evenings, on my own, opening the skylight to evict the deadening heat that builds up in that attic. Sometimes, when it gets too soporific, I go downstairs and sit at my old desk in the silent office, glancing through the window from time to time at the empty market square. I would rather sit there and get some work done than sit alone at home.

I rang David Poe from there one evening, just for a chat. I left a message on his mobile. He hasn't got back to me.

I saw Doug once, in August. He was in the butcher's. I saw him through the window as I passed. The butcher was handing him one of those white translucent bags, bulging with fresh pink mince. They were talking. I hesitated, wondering whether I should go in and say hello, but they seemed engrossed. He was using a stick but other than that he looked well. Everybody thought that Doug would curl up and die after he left his beloved *Record*, but I hear he's doing fine.

I don't make much effort to converse with people these days. I don't even play badminton with Lizzie on Fridays any more – I haven't visited my friends in Birmingham all summer. I dropped in to see my parents once, for half an hour. Mum hardly spoke to me.

I haven't heard from Andrew since he left and don't expect to for a while. I know his silences. I can interpret them. I know when he is not in touch because he is abroad or busy or on drugs – and I know when he is angry with me. It's fine by me because I'm angry back. I don't know why he made such a fuss about Gran's money. He could have had it back any time: all he had to do was ask.

All summer, I have had the sensation that people are avoid-ing me – peculiar, when it is I who am avoiding them.

Nothing much has changed in Nether Bowston. Miss Crabbe

is still working on her masterpiece. She sent a couple of chapters to a publisher in London called the Co-operative Press and they wrote back with a glowing reader's report. They want four thousand pounds to publish but they assure her it will be a huge success. She came round to my place clutching the letter, wanting to know if I thought it was worth it. Apparently, even George Bernard Shaw paid to have his work published. She's very excited.

The village shop is closing. The owner says it's because of the increase in business rates since Independence. I ran a front-page story headlined IS THIS WHAT WE FOUGHT FOR?

The Cowpers' place is up for sale but as yet there are no buyers. I haven't been past it for some time – I have no reason to. It seems strange that the building is still standing. Memories fade, bodies rot, stories become history; but there is still a modern, red-brick monolith on the edge of our village, a far more potent memorial than any gravestone. I can't imagine that anyone would want to live there but apparently some people get a kick out of buying that sort of place. With house prices still rising, property round here is going to be hard to find. Someone will take it.

I think about Gemma sometimes. I think about the photo we ran in the paper, how little it resembled a real girl. That's the trouble with those school pictures. It could be anybody. You look at a photo like that and you think, *dead – so young, and already dead.*

I can't picture what I saw in Ashpit Spinney, not any more. I can picture the yellow roots of the oak tree, the lice and millipedes. I can hear the buzz of the flies. I hear them in my dreams sometimes. They wake me. I sit up, bolt upright, certain that there is a fly in the room, but when my heart has quietened, there is nothing.

Postscript

L ouise Doughty gave herself until she was thirty to be a full time writer. She made it with a week to spare. Eight days before her thirtieth birthday in 1993 she sold her first novel, *Crazy Paving*, on the strength of its opening 100 pages, and signed a contract to write a second, *Dance With Me*.

Crazy Paving was published in 1995 and was shortlisted for four awards, including the John Llewelyn Rhys Prize. *Dance With Me* was published to great critical acclaim in 1996. By the time she came to write *Honey-Dew* in 1997 Doughty was established as an author, radio playwright, critic and broadcaster.

Honey-Dew and the earlier novels share several themes and a bleak sense of humour. *Crazy Paving* was interpreted by many critics as a black comedy. Doughty is, however, anxious that readers don't expect her books to be laugh-out-loud funny. The humour usually comes from bitter situations in everyday life.

All her novels are plot driven. Even though she writes what is categorised as Literary Fiction, the plot always comes first for her. Her skill with plotting is also shown to good effect in her radio plays and she has written several for BBC Radio. She is currently working on a film adaptation of Honey-Dew.

Although Doughty denies there is any autobiography in *Honey-Dew*, she chose to set the novel in Rutland, the county in which she grew up. She believes that there comes a point in any writer's life when they must address their place of birth. Rutland, a land-locked county in the middle of England, is also emblematic for her of a certain kind of Englishness that she wished to explore.

Serious crime was unknown there until 1993 when a man killed his parents and buried them by the side of Rutland Water, a local beauty spot. The Severs Case, as it became known, made national headlines. The case intrigued Doughty and it set her thinking about murder within the family. She wanted to develop the idea that whilst we all have locks on our windows and doors to keep danger out, it is perhaps the darkness within our own homes that we should most fear. With this in mind she decided her story would be about a teenage girl who murders her parents.

Comparing the traditional American and English murder story, Doughty concluded that in general terms the American murder story is about the darkness outside whilst the English version is about murder within a community, by someone from that community. A community such as the one she envisaged in Rutland. She also found, in her reading of everyone from Dorothy L. Sayers to P.D. James, that the traditional crime novel has very strict rules and conventions. Aside from sending up rural England she aimed to subvert these conventions and turn the crime novel on its head by basing the story on the investigator and not the murderer.

Louise Doughty was born in Melton Mowbray but grew up in Oakham, Rutland's county town, one of the three children of an engineer, Ken Doughty, and his wife, Avis. The family were, she says, 'amused bystanders' of the wackier elements of the Seventies campaign for Independence for Rutland.

From an early age she was, she says, 'bookish – definitely a torch under the blankets type when I should have been asleep'. She read voraciously, 'with an absolute passion'. She preferred fantasy and science fiction, 'books that created whole universes you could lose yourself in'.

Academically precocious, Doughty went to Leeds University at the age of seventeen to study English Literature. Although she had always written stories, her ambition then was to be an actress. She had acted at school and continued to do so at university. Her most memorable role was playing one of the eponymous sacks in *Two Sacks*, an obscure drama by an Iranian playwright, but in her final year she realised that she wasn't good enough to make it her career.

Six months of uncertainty followed until she asked herself what she really wanted to do. The realisation that she should write was, she says, like a religious conversion. She eventually applied to do an MA in Creative Writing at the University of East Anglia, and was accepted.

Doughty's contemporaries on the course included writers Anne Enwright and Mark Illis and her tutors were Angela Carter and Malcolm Bradbury, whom she regards as a mentor. Although she doesn't believe a writer can be taught talent, she thinks such courses teach technique and show how talent can be used. She expresses bewilderment that people might think otherwise, since it is accepted that music and art can be taught in a similar way.

Doughty left East Anglia in 1987 and moved to London, where she began a succession of part-time jobs which gave her the freedom to write. In 1991 her first breakthrough came not with the novel but with a short story and a radio play. She won third place – a much-needed £2,000 – in the Ian St James Awards for unpublished writers, with a short story she'd written several years before. Shortly afterwards she came third (and won £500) in the *Radio Times* Drama Awards with a radio play she had adapted from another of her short stories. The play was later broadcast on Radio 3.

Whilst Doughty was writing and winning awards she was also working as a part-time secretary for London Transport. It was her longest lasting part-time job. The experience was dismal but gave her the idea for *Crazy Paving*.

After almost ten years of secretarial work she had become, she says, 'evangelical' about the need to write about sec-retaries since there was, at that pre-Bridget Jones time, no tradition of writing about working women. The 'crystallising factor' came in February 1992 when, now living in Catford and commuting to London Bridge on working days, she narrowly missed being a victim of an IRA bomb that exploded in the railway station.

Such random happenings, combined with a very loose application of chaos theory, provided her with the plot for *Crazy Paving*. (In the book her London Bridge experience figures almost exactly as it happened.) The heroism of 'ordinary' people became one of its themes.

Doughty followed *Crazy Paving* with *Dance With Me*, a ghost story that also examines the relationship between men and women. She wrote in in the daytime before going to the theatre each evening as the critic for the *Mail on Sunday* – a job she had signed up for the day before her thirtieth birthday.

Writing *Dance With Me* was relatively easy. Writing *Honey-Dew* was made more difficult because at the time she was researching it she was pregnant. She gave birth to her daughter Nathalie in November 1996, shortly after she had written the first draft of the first chapter of the book. As a new mother, Doughty found it unsettling to be writing a book about a girl who murders her parents – especially when she stayed with her own parents in Rutland to research it.

She encountered another problem when she went back to Rutland in 1997 for the celebrations to mark the county regaining its old status. She was hoping to get material she could use in the book but found that the celebrations were 'beyond parody'.

It reinforced something she has always believed about writing fiction: 'It is not a question of art imitating life or vice versa. Real life is often far too ludicrous to be rendered literally in fiction. It is more a question of toning it down.'

Peter Guttridge